Return

Richie Leyland

Jean!

Thank you so much!
Enjoy the ride!

Copyright © 2017 by Richie Leyland

All rights reserved.

ISBN: 1546932801
ISBN-13: 978-1546932802

FIRST EDITION

Published by Richie Leyland
www.richieleyland.com

Printed by CreateSpace, An Amazon.com company
Available from Amazon.com and other retail outlets

Cover created by Ryan Mirisoloff
Illustration copyright © 2017 by Ryan Mirisoloff
Used with permission.

This is a work of fiction. Names, characters, places, institutions and incidents either are the product of the author's imagination or are used fictitiously, and any resemblance to actual persons, living or dead, events, or locales is entirely coincidental.

Without limiting the rights under copyright reserved above, no part of this publication may be reproduced, stored in or introduced into a retrieval system, or transmitted, in any form, or by any means (electronic, mechanical, photocopying, recording or otherwise), without the prior written permission of both the copyright owner and the publisher of this book.

I dedicate this story to all of the loved ones I've lost.

ACKNOWLEDGMENTS

I would like to thank all of my family and friends who have been supportive of my creative endeavors throughout my lifetime. I would also like to thank Ryan Mirisoloff for donating his talent to creating the cover of this book. Also, a very special thanks to Lindsay and Pinta. I couldn't have done this without the both of you.

RETURN

ONE

My head hurts. What the hell did I do? It's so damn dark that I can barely see...
"Ah, shit."
I'm upside down.
"I flipped the car."
Well, that's wonderful. Damn deer jumping out at me.
I looked at the driver side and saw a spiderweb of cracks with a little bit of blood. That gave me the indication that I must've hit my head there, hence my newfound pain. I faced towards the windshield and saw that was also broken and punctured with a couple large holes.
Ok, Charlie. Pull it together. Just find the seat belt latch

and get yourself out. Yeah, easier said than done. It's so damn dark in here. Oh, wait, this might be...

"Ow!"

I fell out of the seat and landed on the ceiling, which technically now would be the floor. Dropping out of a car seat like that is more painful than it seems.

Now how do I get out of here? I'll probably have to break out an improvised martial arts move and kick out the cracked window. I just need to get some force behind it... and...

I put my foot through the window with almost no effort.

"Whoa! Huh... that was much easier than I thought it would be."

Alright, you badass. Don't be stupid and cut yourself on these broken shards. You're going to need something to clear the frame. I took off my jacket and wrapped it around my arm.

I need to clear out these pieces so I can fit through the window. Okay, let's have a look.

I stuck my head out of the broken window and looked up. Slopes of dirt and mud surrounded me. I came to the realization that I was at the bottom of a ditch.

I rolled my car into a ditch! Great, my car is probably totaled!

Enough messing around, I'll worry about the car after I squeeze through that damn window. Head out carefully. It looks like there is plenty of space for me to crawl out.

I put my hands in the mud outside of the car to get myself in position. I crawled out through the window slowly. I got all of myself out of the car unscathed then stood up.

Head, arms, legs and feet. I cupped my special parts and breathed a sigh of relief. *I'm all here. I guess I'm all right except for this damn headache.*

I noticed that my left pant leg was torn open. I touched my pockets.

My wallet is gone!

I looked inside the car and did not see it. I searched around the car and I could not find it. It was just mysteriously gone.

The car did not look so good. It was upside down in a ditch with a broken driver side window, a broken windshield, and a warped undercarriage. The front was also crunched like a soda can.

Great. I'm in the middle of nowhere with no car and no money.

I tried to see the silver lining.

"At least it's not on fire."

Well, time for a climb. There has to be something around not too far away. Looking around though, it could be worse. A lot worse. I'll get to the top of this ditch and try to signal someone for help. Scratch that. It looks like I'm in the middle of the woods. I think I'm going to have to walk and bring back help.

Wait a minute.

It's still late. Oh, what time is it? I've been driving around all night. The sun has to be coming up soon.

Where is my phone? I reached into my jacket pocket. I felt my phone. I pulled it out and I saw the giant break on the display. There was no power on the device. *This keeps getting better. Now my phone is smashed.*

Wonderful. What's the next stop on Shit's Creek? Alright, just deal with it and move on to go get help. There has to be something nearby. I began to walk down the road in the direction I was driving and I noticed a stop sign up ahead and the end of the road. *Okay, let's keep moving.* I turned to look behind me and I didn't see any cars around. *I must be way out in the country.* I faced forward and continued walking down the road in my muddy clothes. I reached the stop sign and I looked both ways. *Which way to go, left or right?*

The left looked pretty desolate. I saw dark skies with lots of trees and the road eventually curving into the forest. I turned and looked right. I saw a sign on the road and it said *Return* with an arrow pointing in that direction. It was a straight road also with trees on each side but it looked like there was a very small light at the end.

Maybe it's a way to get back to the highway. Maybe it's not.

"Right, it is." I began to walk down the road.

Well, looks like I will be walking for a while. I need to get to a phone. It's quite a long and quiet road with nothing but trees around. I don't know why I drove so far out into the country. Maybe I should've cleared my head closer to home. I live down the road from a bar. I could've just drank beers and walked home like a normal poor soul drinking away their sorrows, but no; I had to storm out of the apartment and go driving in the heat of the moment. Real smart.

RETURN

Oh, shit. What about Heidi? I bet she hates my guts now. That was the last fight we'll ever have and also the worst one. She broke up with me. I can't call her. I'll call Uncle Greg instead. He can help me out. He's always been there when I've needed him.

This road is much longer than it looks. It just seems to keep going and going. I hope this changes soon. It's so quiet out here that it's unsettling. I figured I would hear animals of some kind but I don't hear anything. My head is throbbing.

How much further to the nearest town? There were so many trees that, actually, it was sort of surreal. It was very picturesque. It was scenery untouched by man. It could have been a Bob Ross painting. The autumn foliage was quite astounding. The oranges and reds were pretty visible in the twilight. The road was also littered with fallen leaves.

Man, my head hurts and now that I'm on my feet, my arm and leg hurt too. At least I'm walking but I have no clue where I am. I've been so distracted with that fight. I don't know how I can make it up to her. I don't even know if she'll let me. She doesn't believe me. She's probably packing up all of her stuff and when I get back, she'll be out of there. I was going to propose to her. That engagement ring is probably pointless to have now.

It started to get easier to see. I wasn't sure if my eyes were adjusting to the environment or if sunrise was approaching. Then I noticed that the sun was finally coming up. Something in the distance captured my gaze.

I see the end of the road! What is that? Is that a town? Fantastic. Let's pick up the pace! Traveling through the woods after a car accident to get to civilization has not been the best way to start the day. I saw a sign up there but the words on it were too small to read from where I was.

I started to advance closer to the sign which I could tell now was illuminated by a small lamp. Buildings were starting to become in view beyond these trees. I started jogging towards the sign to see where exactly I was. As I was nearing the town, I felt waves of pain intensifying in my left leg, left shoulder and the left side of my head. I must've hit this whole side of my body when I rolled the car. I approached the end of the road and I could finally see that sign properly.

Welcome to Return.

"Return? That's kind of an unusual name for a town."
Okay, maybe there's a pay phone or some business open early. Where to go in this town? I decided to go left. I walked towards the next street corner and rounded it. I looked down the road and saw a network of connected brick buildings hosting a wide variety of proprietors. It was a nice looking town. It sort of had a vintage mid-twentieth century appearance to it. It seemed like a very decent place to live and settle down. As I kept staring down the avenue, a diner just a few doors over caught my eye.

"Martha's Diner."
They look open. Good, maybe I can use the phone. I hope I can get something to eat. I'm a bit famished but getting food might be tricky without any money. There were a few cars already moving around in the town and I saw that there were

already people in the diner. *I guess the town gets up early.*

I made my way down the sidewalk and I suddenly felt a little lightheaded. I leaned against a brick wall right next to me. I rested for a moment and breathed slowly to relax myself. After a minute of resting, I felt better and continued towards the diner.

I walked up to the diner and looked inside through the front window. Even the diner looked like it could be from the fifties. Maybe, it could have been older than that. I saw a clock inside and noticed that it was a little bit past seven. I was hoping that maybe I could get a hold of a tow truck.

Well, let's go on in. This is definitely an old school diner. I saw round swirling stools bolted to the floor. The booths had red vinyl upholstery. There was even an old Wurlitzer in the far corner. Pictures of Elvis, Marilyn, and pretty much every other celebrity from that time period adorned the walls.

Wow.

There was an older woman with dark hair styled into a perm wearing a white apron over a yellow T-shirt and jeans behind the counter. I saw her serving coffee to customers at the counter. I was certain she could help me out. The people in here were eating quietly but also looked happy. The food must have been really good.

"Hi, excuse me?", I addressed the waitress. The waitress looked at me and expressed shock. I imagined my appearance caught her off guard.

"Oh my, young man! Are you okay? You look hurt!",

she spoke to me with a concerned tone.

She seems friendly and seems to want to help me.

"I'm okay. Thank you. Do you happen to have a phone I could use? I was in a car accident and my car is in a ditch just outside of town. I need to call for help."

"Of course! I'll meet you down at the end of the counter and show you where it is." She set the pot of coffee on a hot plate and went to go meet me.

I started walking to the far end of the counter and now my head was starting to hurt again, worse than it was before.

"Ow." My equilibrium was shifting and I leaned against the counter. I touched my head and the pain just got more worse. It kept gnawing at me so badly that my vision was starting to get blurry.

My breathing is getting heavy. Something is not right.

"Young man?", said the older woman. "Are you alright? You don't look so well."

"I think I just need to..."

My legs feel weird. Why do I feel so light?

At the moment of feeling that sensation in my legs, I found myself descending and hitting something below. I looked up at the waitress as she was standing over me.

"Oh! Someone go get Laura!", the woman shouted.

Everything became dark. *What's going on?*

TWO

I woke up. *The light is coming back. The diner. The older woman with the perm. The people eating their breakfast. Everyone is looking at me. My head is suddenly cold.*
"Hello? Can you hear me?", asked the woman holding the ice pack to my head. She was dressed in what appeared to be hospital scrubs. "Nod if you can understand me."
I nodded. My vision was slowly coming back and was starting to come into focus and...
Oh my god. She's beautiful. She looks just like Heidi. Except she has reddish brown hair and it's tied up in a bun. Even though, Heidi is a blonde, they look like they could be sisters. The

resemblance is uncanny.

"You passed out and fell. I need you to sit in this booth for a little while and rest. You have quite a nasty gash on the left side of your head here. It also looks like you may have a concussion."

I sat down and grabbed the ice pack from her hand and kept it on my head. *My head hurts like a son of a bitch.*

"I am going to ask you some questions. I'm trying to determine the status of your condition."

"My condition?", I said.

"Well, he speaks. That's a positive sign." She let out a big smile as she looked at me. *Wow, she even smiles like Heidi.*

"Do you know your name?", she asked.

I hesitated for a moment but I remembered.

"My name is Charlie. Charlie Denton."

"Good. Charlie, my name is Laura. I am a nurse and I live in this town. What is my name?"

"Laura..."

"Good, Charlie. Do you remember what happened?"

"I was in a car accident. It happened just outside of town. I walked into town to find a phone. My cell phone was broken in the accident."

"How far did you walk?"

"Not sure. Maybe a mile or two. I walked for a while."

"You sustained a possible concussion and walked a great distance afterwards? No wonder you passed out.", declared Laura. I looked up at Laura.

"Yeah, looking back on that, maybe it was not the best idea but I didn't think anyone would've found me if I stayed where I was. I rolled my car into a ditch." Laura nodded her head slowly like she understood why I walked so far.

The waitress was coming up to the table and she brought a glass of water with her.

"Drink this.", the waitress offered. "You'll feel better."

I drank a few gulps of water from the glass and set it back down on the table. I didn't realize how thirsty I was.

"Thank you, Martha.", said Laura.

"Yes, thank you. I'm sorry for passing out in your diner."

"No need to apologize. Let's just focus on you being all right.", Martha advised. Martha went back to the counter and poured some coffee for the patrons sitting at the counter. Plates of food were coming out to those customers and those wonderful breakfast aromas were infiltrating my nostrils.

Laura picked up the glass of water and handed it back to me. "Drink the whole thing. It will help you.", she suggested. I took the glass and swallowed the remaining water. "Do you remember how the accident happened?", she inquired.

"I remember that it was raining and a deer jumped out at me."

I had to think for a moment but some more details came back to me.

"I swerved to avoid the deer but after that, the next thing I remember is that I woke up hanging upside down from my seat." When I finished my explanation, she stuck her index finger in the air. "Keep your eyes on my finger.", she commanded.

I watched her finger moved back and forth as she stared intently into my eyes. "Your eyes look OK", she stated, "but I would like to take you to the hospital here in town and have a look at your head with some equipment there."

I exhaled and rubbed my head with the ice pack. I still felt lightheaded. I responded back, "If you think that's best, then I won't debate it. Can we wait a little bit? I'm not ready to move yet."

"Sure", she said. "Are you hungry? I'm sure some food will help."

As Laura said this, Martha approached the table.

"You should eat up, Darlin'. Breakfast is the most important meal of the day.", commented Martha.

"I am hungry but I don't know if I could keep down eggs, bacon and toast with coffee. I feel a little nauseated. Also, I lost my wallet so I can't pay you."

"Don't worry about that.", said Laura.

"I got just the thing for you. I'll bring you a bowl of my homemade and famous chicken noodle soup. I know it may be a little early for soup but trust me, it works wonders.", suggested Martha. Laura added, "It is excellent and it'll help."

"Sounds good. I'll take a bowl of your famous chicken noodle soup. Could I get another glass of water as well, please?", I asked.

"Of course.", Martha replied. "Laura, would you like anything?"

"A little bowl of fruit, one poached egg, and two

pieces of wheat toast with orange marmalade.", answered Laura. "Very good. I'll bring those out to both of you shortly.", Martha said as she scribbled down our order and walked back to the kitchen.

"So, Charlie. That's a nice name. You can tell a lot by a person just by their name. Do you know what it means?", asked Laura.

"It is derived from a Germanic word meaning 'man.' There is also another theory that it originated from the Germanic element 'hari', which means 'warrior.'", I replied.

"Very good. Do you know what Laura means?", she tested me.

"The laurel tree symbolic of honor and victory."

"Very good!", she exclaimed. She sounded impressed.

"How do you know so much about etymology?", I asked.

"I've always found it to be interesting. It's kind of remarkable how a name can shape you as a person. How about you?"

"Well, I'm no expert on the subject but I pretty much have that interest for the same reasons."

She's smart and beautiful. I like her.

Martha approached the table and brought over our glasses of water. She went back to the kitchen. I took a few more gulps of water and I slowly felt this fog that was over me starting to lift.

"Thank you for helping me.", I remarked. "In the world today, it seems like the kindness of strangers is far and few between."

Laura said, "In the world, yes. Here, it's a little different. We're a pretty well knit community. About a little bit under four thousand people live here but everyone pretty much knows each other. All of us are just trying to get by and when necessary, we help each other out."

"I've lived in New York State my entire life. I've never heard of this town. Where exactly are we?", I questioned her as I set the ice pack down on the table.

"Actually, we are on the edge of the state. There's a great lake immediately north of us that's only a couple miles away."

Martha was coming back to the table with our food. She set the bowl of soup in front of me then placed the plate of toast and the poached egg along with the bowl of fruit in front of Laura.

"Here you go, you two. Enjoy!", said Martha. Martha left us and headed back to the counter to pour some more coffee for the customers at the counter. The soup in front of me smelled so good. Laura spread the orange marmalade on her toast and bit into it with such satisfaction. I took a spoonful of noodles and chicken and put the spoon in my mouth. I felt that tasty broth and hearty chicken going into my stomach and it was unbelievable.

"Oh, wow."

"It's pretty great, right?", implied Laura.

"It's amazing. This may be the best bowl of chicken noodle soup I've ever had. I don't think I've ever had a bowl this delicious, well since, my mother would make it."

"Oh yeah? Is your mom a really good cook?"

RETURN

"Well, she was. Both my parents died when I was 12 years old.", I replied.

Laura stopped eating for a moment and looked at me with sorrow. "I'm sorry to hear that, Charlie."

"It's okay but thank you. I just turned 30 last month so it's been a long time. So when that happened my Uncle Greg took on the task of raising me. He's my father's younger brother and he's been there for me ever since. I was an only child, so my uncle and I are pretty close."

"Gregory is a fitting name for your uncle."

"Watchful. Indeed, it is."

"What were your parents' names?"

"Nicholas and Cynthia. Also, good and strong names.", I divulged. "The victory of the people and the famous bearer. I agree completely.", affirmed Laura.

"How about you? Tell me about your family.", I asked. I went back to devouring that soup like it was my last meal.

"My mother died over ten years ago right before I entered my senior year of high school.", Laura told me.

She lost a parent, too.

"I'm sorry for your loss.", I sympathized.

"Thank you. She had a brain tumor and it's what sparked my interest in health and medicine. Now, it's just my father and I, and our farm. I'm also an only child so you can imagine how close my father and I are. He thinks he takes care of me but really I do all the heavy lifting." She winked at me and smiled. At that moment, that made me smile and my mood was slowly getting better.

Martha came up to the table and dropped the check down in front of Laura. Laura picked up the check and looked at it. "Like I said before, don't worry about breakfast. I got it.", she insisted. "Again, thank you.", I replied. I was grateful. She dropped the check back on the table and threw down a ten dollar bill and a couple singles.

"Alright, are you feeling any better? Can you walk for a bit?", Laura asked. "Yeah, I'm a little better.", I informed her. "Good, then I'm taking you to the hospital. I'm going to have a doctor look at your head."

"Okay nurse, let's go."

Laura smirked at me then turned around and yelled towards the kitchen. "Martha, we're all set. Have a good one." Martha projected back, "You too, Laura. Charlie, it was nice to meet you. Hope to see you again."

"Thank you for the soup, Martha. It was out of this world."

"Anytime, Darlin'.", Martha responded.

Laura and I got up from the booth and I was able to maintain my balance on my feet. I put the ice pack back on my head and we walked out the door. We walked up to her red pickup truck that was parked a few spots over. As I was approaching the truck, I noticed a guy on the sidewalk with a worn out hat and a beard wearing a shirt that looked like it had some fish on the front. The thing is that I noticed that it seemed like he was giving me a dirty look. I looked back at him, confused.

"Who's that guy?", I asked. Laura looked at him and

then looked right back at me. "Oh, great.", she sighed and then turned her back on the man. It sounded and looked like she didn't want to see him.

"Hey, Laura.", addressed the man. I saw Laura clench her face then relax it and she turned around.

"Hi, Tyler.", she responded back. It sounded like she was trying to be as polite and curt as she could be.

"Who's your friend?", Tyler asked.

I looked at him and introduced myself, "Hi, I'm Charlie." I waved at him with my free hand.

"I wasn't talking to you, *Charlie*.", he snapped back in a rude manner. I was a little lost by why he got irritated with me. *Maybe it was a misunderstanding.*

"Tyler!" cried Laura. "I don't want you starting anything."

"Nobody's starting anything. I'm just saying 'hi'. That's all.", Tyler said calmly. Laura exhaled deeply.

"You both have a nice day.", he said sternly. Then he turned around and walked away. He looked over his shoulder back at us, then turned forward again and kept walking down the sidewalk. I looked back at over Laura. "Come on. Get in.", she sighed.

We both got in the truck. I sat in the passenger seat and fastened my seat belt. It saved me last time. Laura started up the truck, backed up out of the parking spot then drove down the road and into the center of town. We drove into a very wide open area of the town with a large park in the middle.

Analyzing the town square more closely, I just noticed

how huge it really was. It seemed more like a rectangle considering that it looked like the size of a football field. Although, it seemed larger than that. I saw shops, food establishments and other local businesses that surrounded the area. I saw that this was a very active part of the town. "This is the town square even though it's more of a rectangle as you can see. Calling it the town rectangle doesn't roll off the tongue as easily.", she joked. I cracked a smile. "The hospital is just past this road over here.", she explained.

"So who's Tyler?", I asked.

Laura sighed again.

"It's okay if you don't want to talk about it."

"No, it's perfectly fine.", she assured me. "He's an ex-boyfriend. We dated for almost a couple years and we broke up about three years ago. It did not end well."

"Makes sense why you wouldn't want to speak with him. Are you alright? How badly did it end?"

"Well, it definitely did not end on a good note but it could've been much worse. He has a temper and loves his whiskey way too much. One night, he got very physical and that was the limit. I couldn't handle it anymore."

"Understandable.", I said in agreement.

"Plus, my father was ready to kick the shit out of him. I had to stop that from happening, too.", Laura added.

I looked at her and let a small grin slip. She noticed and grinned back at me.

"Well, if it makes you feel better, I also know another asshole named Tyler.", I confessed.

She laughed at my little quip and that seemed to

break the tension.

"It does a bit. Thanks.", she joked back.

I wasn't lying about what I said. Heidi's ex-boyfriend is named Tyler. Well, that would be her previous ex-boyfriend. Technically, I would currently be her ex-boyfriend.

Laura pulled into the hospital parking lot, parked the truck and killed the engine. We stepped out and I followed her lead across the parking lot. "This way, we'll take the back entrance.", she commanded. I followed her around the corner and we approached a wide electronic door. The door slid open and we entered the hospital.

THREE

    I was laying inside a CT machine with a hospital gown on. I heard the humming and whirring of the scanner. I kept thinking about how I was going to fix my mess. It was an overwhelming pile of crap but I knew that I had to have the mindset to just take care of one thing at a time because I'm only human.
    "Ok, Charlie. We're done.", said Laura over the intercom. The bed extracted out of the machine and it stopped. I sat up and I touched the fresh bandage on my head. I looked in the window and saw that Laura was now wearing a sweatshirt but still wearing her scrub pants. The

MRI technician got up from her chair and exited the observing room. Laura walked through the door into my room and walked up to me. I started putting my clothes back on.

"Oh, I'm sorry." She turned around.

"It's okay. I'm not shy but you can look now.", I assured her. She turned back around and I already had my torn pants back on.

"I'm no doctor but I've seen enough of these to have a basic understanding. The scan looked alright. She's going to get the doctor." Immediately after when Laura said that, I saw the technician walk back into the observing room with the doctor. He was analyzing my scan pretty intensely. I started to feel a little nervous from watching the doctor work but Laura seemed relaxed. Having her here with me became very comforting and the anxiety was slowly disappearing.

"Hey, do you happen to have a phone by any chance? I know I'm going to have to make some calls after we're done here.", I said.

"I called a tow truck to get your car. They are on their way there now.", she replied.

"Great. I do need to call my Uncle though and just let him know I am okay and that I'm stranded out here."

The doctor walked in the room and approached us.

"Laura. How are you?", the doctor enthusiastically said.

"I'm good, Doc. How about you?"

"I'm wonderful. You on the clock?"

"No, I got off of the late shift a little bit ago. I went to

Martha's for breakfast and he collapsed in the diner." The doctor looked over at me.

"You must be Charlie. Hi, I'm Dr. Watkins."

"Hi, Doc. Nice to meet you. How's it looking?", I asked.

"Well, Charlie. You took a good bump on the head. You might need a couple stitches for the wound but other than some swelling, your scan looked clean.", explained Dr. Watkins.

"Well, that's good news, right?", I asked.

"Yes, it's great news. It could've been much worse. However, you should take it easy for the next few days so you do not aggravate your condition. Bed rest with plenty of water for the next four, five days. Take Ibuprofen to reduce the swelling or relieve any pain if necessary. Doctor's orders." He handed me a note, along with a prescription, explaining my condition and that I needed to rest. It was signed by him.

"Ok, Doc. Thank you.", I responded back.

"Sure. Why don't you have a seat and I'll take a closer look at that wound for you.", he instructed. I sat down in a nearby chair. He went up to a rolling chest and pulled it towards Laura and me. The doctor also pulled up a stool. He sat down on the stool and opened a drawer from the rolling chest. He pulled out a pair of gloves and put them on. He pulled the bandage off of my head and examined the wound.

"Alright, Charlie just hold on for a couple minutes.", he advised me.

RETURN

He went over to the rolling chest and he pulled out some thread and a needle and placed both objects on the top of the chest.

"Hold still, Charlie.", the doctor commanded.

I sat motionless in the chair. The doctor pulled out a cotton swab from the open drawer. He soaked the swab with a solution of some kind and I felt him clean the wound. Afterwards, he threw the swab on top of the chest. He picked up the needle and thread from the top of the chest then fed the thread through the eye of the needle and secured it. I felt the needle prick my skin and then felt him run the thread through the wound. He guided the needle through my skin one more time and tugged on the thread. He took a pair of scissors from the drawer and cut the thread. The doctor then set the scissors down on the top of the chest. He finally pulled a new bandage out of the drawer and put it over the wound.

"All done.", he said. He put the tools back in the drawer. He got up from the stool and threw the gloves in the trash.

"That's it?", I asked.

"That's it. Just two stitches.", the doctor clarified.

"Thank you. That was very easy.", I told him.

"No problem.", he said. He looked over at Laura and then back at me. "Laura, I'll see you around. You both have a good day." Dr. Watkins exited the room.

Laura looked at me and smiled. "See, I told you it would be alright.", she said to me with a smile on her face. I smiled back at her then took the gown off and put my shirt back on. When I had all of my clothes back on, I took a good look at myself and realized how dirty I was and how dirty my clothes were. I had so much mud and dirt on them, probably from climbing out of the car, and no extra clothes with me. I turned around and looked at the back of my pant leg where it was torn open. "Damn. I liked these jeans. I'm filthy. I bet I stink too."

"Don't worry. I won't hold it against you.", she quipped. She smiled at me. That made me chuckle. *She is funny. I like her.*

"Come with me. I'll give you a ride to my place. You can use our shower.", she insisted. I grabbed my jacket, which was also dirty and a little torn up and I followed her out the door.

We were exiting the hospital and Laura's phone rang. She pulled the phone out of her pocket and looked at the caller ID. "It's the tow truck company.", she said. She answered the phone. "Hello?" I heard talking on the other end but couldn't understand what was being said. "Yes. Hi, Rick. What's up?"

I heard more talking which I couldn't make out. It sounded like some big explanation. "Here, let me put him on the phone." She looked at me and handed the phone to me. "You should talk to him." I took the phone from her.

"Hello, this is Charlie Denton."

"Hi, Mr. Denton. This is Rick from Return Towing and Repair. We found your car in the ditch but I'll level with you, it's totaled."

"Totaled?!"

"Yeah, the broken windows and dents on the side and roof are only the top of the cake. Your front axle is broken, the gas tank has been punctured, the engine block has been cracked and one of the pistons has blown. It's an older car so it would cost more to get it fixed than what it's worth."

Ah, hell. I liked that car.

"Great. So how much is this service going to cost me?", I asked.

"I'll tell you what, Mr. Denton. Laura seems to like you very much if she's doing this for you and we have great respect and appreciation of her and Henry, so I'll strip the car for parts and we'll waive the fee for the tow."

"Deal.", I agreed.

"Sounds good.", said Rick. "Could you put Laura back on the phone, please?"

"Sure and thank you."

"No problem and thank you.", said Rick. I handed the phone back to Laura. Laura took the phone from me.

"Hello?"

More talking that I could not understand. Laura chuckled.

"I will tell him. Thanks, Rick. I'll talk to you. Bye." She hung up the phone and shook her head but seemed upbeat about it.

"Who's Henry?", I asked.

"Henry is my father.", she answered.

"Ah. Sounds like you know everyone here."

"For the most part, yeah." She smiled at me again.

I loved it when she smiled.
"Rick wanted me to tell you…"
I focused on her.
"…that you sound more friendly than Tyler."
I chuckled and then she did too.
"I'll take that as a compliment.", I said. Laura laughed. We got to her truck then I remembered that I needed to call Uncle Greg. "Oh yeah, could I borrow your phone please?"
"Sure." She handed me her phone again. I dialed my uncle's cell phone. I heard it ring and then it went to voice mail.

"Hello. You've reached the voice mail of Gregory Denton. I'm currently out of the country on business so please leave a message and I will get back to you at my earliest convenience."

The greeting beeped.
"Uncle Greg, it's Charlie. Listen, I was just involved in a car accident. I'm this town called 'Return.' People here have been helping me out but I need someone to come pick me up. A doctor looked at me and I suffered a concussion. I was ordered bed rest and to take it easy. So if you could, please get back to me."
I looked at Laura and whispered "What's your number?"
She replied, "716…"
"The number is 716…"
"525-4365."
"…525-4365."

RETURN

"You can stay at the farm if necessary. We have an extra room out in the barn.", she mentioned.

I continued on with my message. "I met a very friendly lady who has been helping me out. She's offering me to stay with her temporarily. Her name is Laura, so that number is for her phone. I'll talk to you soon, Uncle Greg. Love you." I hung up the phone and gave it back to Laura.

"His voice mail stated that he is out of the country on the business."

"Then it's settled. You're staying with me until he can come get you.", she demanded.

"Are you sure that's okay?", I asked. "What about your father?"

"It'll be fine. He can't do shit about it. Legally, I own half of the farm."

"Can't do shit about it, huh?"

She chuckled. "Does the cursing bother you?"

I chuckled harder. "No, not at all. In fact, I don't trust people who don't swear. If you don't swear, you're not an honest person."

"Shit, yeah.", she said. We both got into her truck and she started the vehicle. She pulled out of the parking lot and turned right out into the street. She turned right around another corner and continued straight down the road as less buildings were around and more wooded areas began to appear.

We were heading away from the town and as we advanced up the road, I slowly saw the horizon developing and I saw nothing but water. It was a great lake alright. It had an intimidating beauty to it. It made me feel uneasy but I was still mesmerized by what I saw. Off in the distance to my left, there was an old white lighthouse that was very tall. Right when I was starting to admire the lighthouse, Laura slowed down and made a sharp right turn into a dirt and gravel driveway accompanied with a mailbox in the shape of a large airplane.

    I saw a big red brick house with a massive red barn. There was a fence attached to the barn and I saw a lone horse within the perimeter of the fence. There were some wide open fields and the property was surrounded by the woods. I noticed a large green tractor working out in the fields and I saw various vegetation along the property. *My guess is that they are crops of some kind.*

    "We're here.", she announced. She stopped the truck, put it in park, and turned off the engine. We got out and walked up to the front porch. We stepped onto the wooden porch and I saw two rocking chairs that were accompanied with an uprooted tree stump that seemed to be used as a table. She opened the door for me and we headed into the house.

FOUR

I stepped out of the shower feeling rejuvenated. My head was still hurting like a bastard. I wiped the mirror and I took a closer look at my face.
I could use a shave.
I lifted the bandage and looked at the wound on the left side of my head. There were two stitches holding the cut closed. The wound was a profoundly red slit against my light olive skin. "Hard to believe that something this small would feel like my head being crushed.", I thought out loud to myself. I stuck the bandage back to my skin. A bottle of mouthwash was sitting on the sink and I picked it up. I

opened the bottle and took a swig of mouthwash then swished it in my mouth. There was a pair of knocks on the door.

"Hey", Laura said through the door. "I brought you some clothes. They are sitting on the chair outside here."

I opened the door with the towel around my waist, still swishing the mouthwash in my mouth. I saw them on the chair and went to pick them up. As soon as I grabbed the clothes, I heard an older and gruff voice with a strange familiarity to me say, "Those sweat pants have a drawstring around the waist if they are too big for you." I looked in the direction of where the voice was coming from and saw a very muscular cowboy. He had some dirt on his shirt and jeans. There were salt and pepper patterns in his stubble and gray shades of wisdom above his ears slowly fading into the dark shade of hair on top of his head. When I looked at his face more carefully, he was a dead ringer for this one action movie star. This threw me off so instantaneously that I ended up prematurely spitting out the mouthwash into the clothes, probably his clothes, that Laura just gave me.

I briefly panicked.

I look like an idiot. I just did this stupid thing to my hosts, in front of a woman I like and a guy who would probably kick my ass for wearing only a towel in front of his daughter.

"I'm sorry. I just, uh, I don't know what I was doing or what happened. I'm sorry.", I blurted out.

"You must be Charlie.", he said.

"Yes, sir. I'm guessing you're Henry.", I replied.

He nodded firmly and calmly but didn't seem mad or

irritated. His arms were crossed and he stared at me with blazing focus. I looked over at Laura and she was quietly chuckling to herself. "There's a room in the barn with a bed and some blankets. You can stay out there for the time being. There is also a toilet out there but the only shower is right behind you. I start working at 6 every morning. I like my sleep. I also love my daughter very much. Are we on the same page?", said Henry.

"Yes, sir.", I promptly answered.

"Good." Henry turned around and exited the room. I heard the sound of his boots moving further away and heard the front door open then close.

"I'm sorry. I know he's intimidating. He's just looking after me because I'm his little girl.", Laura added.

"Hey, did anyone ever tell you that he looks like..."

"Stop.", interrupted Laura. "I know who you are going to say. Don't ever say that to him. He does not like it."

I was surprised by this.

"Okay. I won't bring it up again.", I told her. Laura grabbed the newly spoiled clothes from me. "Here I'll take those and get you some more clothes. You finish getting cleaned up." She cracked a smile and walked into the other room. I went back into the bathroom and closed the door. I put my hands on the sink and looked in the mirror. I exhaled with profound depth.

"At least, my towel didn't fall off."

Another knock on the door.

"New clothes on the chair for you.", Laura said. I heard footsteps move away from the door. I opened the bathroom door and there was another sweat suit on the chair. I was perfectly fine with that.

The weather is getting colder now and I need some rest so I might as well be comfortable.

I brought in the clothes and put them on. These pants also had a drawstring around the waist and I definitely needed to adjust these pants.

Henry is a big guy.

I walked out of the bathroom in my new attire, holding the damp towel in my hands.

"Laura?", I called out.

"Yeah?", she called back.

"What do you want me to do with this towel?"

"The laundry room is next to the bathroom. Immediately to your right when you enter is a hamper. Put the towel in there, please."

I followed her instructions, found the hamper and dropped the towel into the hamper. I walked out of the laundry room and into the kitchen where I found Laura. She was filling a pitcher with water. She turned off the faucet, covered the pitcher and grabbed a plastic cup from the cupboard above her. She closed the cupboard and then looked at me.

"Follow me. I'll show you to your bed.", she instructed.

We walked out the front door and walked over to the left side of the barn, which was the side without the fence, and arrived at a white door on the side. Laura opened the door and it opened into a small living space with another rocking chair and small sofa. There was a book shelf nearly at capacity against the wall opposite the sofa. There was also a small table next to the rocking chair and a small trash can next to the table. On the table, I saw a copy of *To Kill A Mockingbird*. I pointed at the book.

"Good book.", I said.

"It's a great book. I read it in school and I've read it a few more times since then.", she admitted.

"I read it in school, too."

Laura took me around a corner on my left and into a small hallway. There was an open door on my right, which had only a toilet and a sink. We went through the closed door on the left and there was a queen size bed with a wooden frame. The sunlight from the small sliding window was projecting on to the center of the bed. There was a nightstand next to the bed with an alarm clock and a small lamp. Positioned on my left was a dresser against the wall and a mirror next to the dresser. Laura set down the pitcher and the plastic cup on the dresser. She opened a small closet and pulled out an extra blanket. She tossed the blanket onto the bed and shut the closet.

"Okay, that should be good for now. Bathroom is across the hall. Dinner is usually ready around 5 but I'll come check on you later to see how you are."

"Sounds good. Thank you again."

"It's not a problem. Besides, you seem like a good person and I know you need the help right now."

She was right. I did need the help.

"Get some rest because I need sleep too." She smiled

at me and exited the room.

"Thank you.", I called out.

"You're welcome.", she shouted back. Then I heard the front door close.

I unwrapped the bed sheets and the blanket. I tucked myself in and put the blanket on top of me. This pillow was so soft against the back of my head. I felt heavy and then I became calm.

I was replaying the events of the accident in my head but the details were still foggy. I remember the argument, Heidi breaking it off with me, leaving her behind at the apartment, the time I spent driving, the giant buck appearing in the middle of the road, and me swerving off of the road.

That's it. That's all I can remember. I can't be stressing out about this more than I have to be. Heidi is not a part of my life anymore. She doesn't want me. I need to get over it. Laura has been very helpful and very nice and it's quite unbelievable how she looks so much like Heidi. It just makes me nervous. She even has a fit body just like Heidi. I just need to get by for the next week or so, hopefully it won't be that long, without trying to piss off Henry or Laura. I'm not used to charity like this. I hope Uncle Greg isn't gone long. I need to let my thoughts stop racing or I won't fall asleep.

I focused on picturing a clear night sky in my head. I thought of stars painted on the vast backdrop of space and the shape of the moon protruding at me with a glow of permanence. I felt myself relaxing more and then darkness consumed me.

    I woke up.
It was dark. I looked out the window and saw that it was now night time. I still felt tired. I went to the bathroom and relieved myself. After finishing, I flushed, washed my hands and came back into the bedroom. I poured myself some water and drank it in one large gulp as if I was returning from the desert. I put down the cup then looked out the window again and saw it was a clear and starry night. It was almost like how I pictured the sky in my head. My view from the window also saw that horizon as we were driving up to Laura's house earlier.
    I turned around and went back to bed. As soon as I got comfortable, I heard the front door open. I heard footsteps approaching the bedroom door and it opened.
    "Charlie?", said Laura.
    "Yep,", I mumbled.
    "How are you feeling?"
    "Still tired but okay for now."
    "Good. I'm about to take the night shift but wanted to see if you needed anything before I go. Are you hungry?", she said.
    "Not really. I don't think I need anything. I'm just going to try and get more rest."
    "Okay, I'll come check on you again tomorrow morning when I get home."
    "Thank you."

Laura closed the door gently. The footsteps got quieter and the darkness consumed me again.

Those pieces of my memories were flashing by again. I tried to think of that clear night sky again. I slept.

I woke up.

My head was throbbing less. I went to the bathroom then came back to the bedroom and I saw that it was still night. I poured myself another glass of water and downed the whole thing. I laid back in bed then I heard the door creak open and could sense someone behind it.

"Charlie, are you okay? Do you need anything?", Laura asked.

My face was partially in the pillow.

"No, I'm fine. I'm just tired. I don't need anything right now. Thanks.", I said. I didn't know what it was but I felt like I couldn't get enough sleep.

"Okay, don't be afraid to come get me if you need anything.", she said.

"Okay." I heard the door close gently.

Suddenly, I thought of Martha's chicken noodle soup. Even though I wasn't very hungry, the thought of having a bowl of that right now seemed good. I imagined the diner and as I was walking in, Martha waved at me with a big smile on her face. I sat down at the counter and there was a gentleman with his back to me behind the counter wearing an apron.

"Excuse me, could I get a bowl of the chicken noodle

soup?", I asked.
>He turned around and it was my Uncle Greg.
>"Uncle Greg?"
>"We don't serve soup here. Wake up.", he said. He took a rolled up newspaper and hit me on the left side of my head.

>I woke up.
>I looked up and I saw Laura.
>She was standing there holding a tray of food looking concerned.
>"Are you okay? You were tossing and turning a bit."
>I was still a little shocked by what just happened but then I finally got the words out.
>"Yes, I'm fine. Weird dream. Did you bring me breakfast in bed?" I felt my appetite come back.
>"I did!", she happily said.
>"Oh, my. Thank you so much! I've never had breakfast in bed before." I sat up and she put the tray down over my legs so it was sitting just above my lap like a table. There were eggs, bacon, hash browns, toast with strawberry jam and butter, along with a little dish of blueberries and raspberries along with some coffee and orange juice.
>*Whoa. She put some love into this meal.*
>"This is awesome and it looks amazing.", I said.
>*I think I am starting to fall for her. Oh, boy. Is this the Florence Nightingale effect but reversed?*
>"Thank you. You're very kind.", she smiled back at me.
>I took my fork and dug into the meal. It was so

delicious. It felt like I hadn't eaten in days. Every bite was heavenly. The coffee was fresh. The orange juice was squeezed with pieces of pulp. The eggs, hash browns and bacon were cooked to perfection.

"Oh, this is so good!", I exclaimed. This meal was starting to lift my spirits and physically I felt better.

"I'm glad you like it. I left you this morning's paper on your night stand." She pointed to the stand and I saw the paper.

"Also, your uncle called my phone and left a voice mail.", said Laura.

She pressed a button on the phone and handed the phone to me. We heard my uncle's voice on the other end.

"Charlie, I got your message. I'm in London for another week but I may be able to get there sooner. I will call you as soon as I am back in the States. I got this number but if you run into an emergency, I'm sure you could call Heidi."

I shifted uncomfortably and let out a sigh when he said her name. *He doesn't know what happened.* The message continued.

"I'll bring you back a souvenir. Love you, pal. I'll talk to you soon." The message ended. I gave the phone back to Laura.

She looked at me and said, "So, who's Heidi?"
No point in keeping it from her.
I sighed and slightly shook my head.
"She is my ex-girlfriend. We were together for nearly three years."

Laura looked a little puzzled.
"If she is your ex, then why would he suggest calling

her?"

"He doesn't know that we broke up. We broke up the other night shortly before I had my accident. It was a very bad breakup. I can't call her."

"Oh... well, I guess that does make sense.", she said.

"Yep...", I trailed off and couldn't think of anything to say to that. I took a bite of bacon. I reached over for the newspaper and my eyes grew with shock as I swallowed hard.

The date of the paper said Wednesday, November 6th.
It was Sunday morning when I went to sleep!
I slept for three days?!

FIVE

"Oh, shit! I need to call my boss! I didn't think I would've slept this long!" I panicked. Laura immediately handed me her phone.
"Thank you.", I said.
I dialed the number for my place of employment and I was currently concerned if it would become my former place of employment. The phone rang and then I heard someone pick up on the other line.
"Red Wheel Products. This is Shirley."
"Shirley, it's Charlie. Is Dean there?"
"Charlie, he's in his office.", answered Shirley. Then I heard yelling behind her over the phone. "I'm going to

transfer you to him. Hold on." She transferred the call. I heard the phone pick up on the other end.

"Charlie..."

He sounded pissed.

"... where the hell have you been?!"

"Dean, I'm sorry. I was in a car accident. This is the first time I've been able to get to a phone after the emergency.", I answered back.

"I don't give a shit! You were supposed to be here on Monday to give the presentation!"

"Dean, I'm sorry! I didn't plan on being in the car accident! I'm stuck in another town and I even have a doctor's note ordering me to get some rest."

"Yeah, more excuses. You're fired, Charlie. We'll mail you your shit.", he fired back.

"I swear I'm telling the truth!"

Then I thought about what I really wanted to say.

What kind of person acts this way towards someone who's been through an ordeal like this?

"You know what, Dean? Fuck you. I work hard at my job. You treat your employees like shit. I told you the truth and you refuse to listen. I would rather not work with anyone like that. Any boss that verbally abuses his employees is not a leader or a motivator... and any boss that runs a business that way will burn it to the ground. I gotta go. Fuck you." I hung up the phone and gave it back to Laura. She had a look of shock on her face that slowly turned into a smile.

"That... was seriously fucking awesome.", she said.

I had a good laugh and then my head started to hurt.

I had to rest for a moment. The pain wasn't as intense as it was the other day. However, the way she made me feel good about myself was worth the pain I had to experience. It felt good to say all of that to Dean as well. I didn't care if he gave me a bad reference. I've got some work stories about him that are slightly disturbing. *What's done is done.*

It was time to move past that so I just looked at Laura and I felt perfectly content. *Wow. Her eyes even look like Heidi's.* I noticed she was in her scrubs.

"Just getting off of a shift?", I asked her.

"Yes, and I'm off until next Monday!", she expressed with lots of joy.

"Oh yeah? For that long?", I asked.

"Yep, I'm going to be helping around the festival on Saturday."

"What festival?"

"It's the Return Heritage Festival. It's an anniversary celebration of the town that occurs in the very large town square we passed by on the way to the hospital. Saturday, the town turns 200 years old."

"Wow. 200 years?!" I stood up on both of my feet. I felt good and my head pain had quickly faded.

"Hey, are you feeling better?", she asked. "You look better."

"I am and thank you.", I replied.

I started walking around to get the blood flowing and the pins and needles out of my legs. After I started to feel my legs wake up, then I went to the bathroom. I did my duty and saw that Laura put a toothbrush and a tube of toothpaste on the sink. I brushed my teeth and removed the bandage from my head. The wound on my head looked fine so I decided to let it breathe and I tossed the soiled material in the trash. When I exited the bathroom, Laura brought back some of Henry's clothes and a pair of boots for me that were sitting on the dresser. The boots looked like they might fit. I do have big feet. I also saw my jacket hanging on the back of a chair in the room. She cleaned it up. I smiled at her and thanked her.

"Your dad is double my size. I don't think those clothes are going to fit me.", I said.

"These are some of his older clothes that do not fit him anymore. Take a look. I have a feeling.", she said then exited the bedroom with the tray. Before she left out of the front door, she turned around with the tray and said, "Hey, I'm going to take a nap. I'm pretty exhausted after that last shift but feel free to look around the town if you start to feel stir crazy."

"Thanks, I may do that. Get some rest.", I said.

She smiled at me then turned around and walked out the door.

I went back into the bedroom and examined the clothes. I picked up the pair of jeans and looked at the measurements. These would fit me. I checked out the T-shirt; I put it on and it fit me very well. There was also a nice casual dress shirt. I tried that and it fit but I decided to stay with the T-shirt for now and wear my jacket.

How about the boots? Size 12. Alright, all of these would

fit.

I finished dressing in the clothes and then stepped outside with my jacket on. It was very sunny and comfortable outside for early November in New York State. I determined that I didn't need the jacket. It was too warm. I took it off and walked back inside. I tossed it back in the room and onto the rocking chair.

I closed the door and walked away from the barn. The sky was extremely clear and the sun was beaming strongly upon me as I started to walk down the driveway and onto the road into town. I looked back at Laura's property and I saw a large green tractor moving down a field. I couldn't tell if it was Henry but I figured it had to be.

I stayed on the road as it was a straight shot right to the town square. I could just make it out that I could see the center of town from where I was. There weren't many houses on this block. It was mostly woods and fields. I reached an intersection. I walked across the street and over to the next block. There were more houses and I saw a woman walking her dog approaching me.

"Hello there!", she said.

"Hi.", I said casually and she just kept walking by me.

People are pretty friendly in this town. Well, except for Tyler but I assume there is probably more to that story that I do not know.

I kept on my journey and the town square was becoming more visible. I walked by a gas station and saw attendants filling up cars for customers. *That's something you don't see much of these days.*

Before I knew it, I finally got to the town square. It wasn't a long walk. I saw the wide open town square and I really did not notice just how large it was at first glance. There were some carnival rides slowly being set up. I saw a small blimp on the very large patch of grass in the very center of the town square. I also saw a couple of hot air balloons. It had just occurred to me that I have not seen a blimp or a hot air balloon up close before except for in photographs.

I looked across the street and over to my right and I saw the town library. I decided to go check that out. I looked both ways; I saw that traffic was light, and I crossed the road. As I was crossing the town square, I noticed something in the park that looked kind of odd but really piqued my curiosity.

It was an iron box secured to a thick iron pole that was about four feet tall that stuck in the ground. The box itself was about two feet long, roughly a foot and a half wide and maybe close to a foot and a half tall. I noticed a perfect circle on the top center of the box that had a lighter metallic shade from the rest of the box.

On the front of the box were eight metallic spinning dials with big engraved numbers. I turned some of the dials and it appeared that each dial had numbers 0 through 9. I looked around the box and I did not see any hinges. Every side of the chest was flat and void of any distinct characteristics except for the side with the dials. Below the chest was a sign that read:

"In Loving Memory of the founder of Return, Jeffrey Fitzgerald Hammond, at his request, we place this key to the universe here so any lost soul may find their way home."

In front of the box was a small stone plinth. The plinth had an engraving in the top with the following text:

THIS IS THE KEY TO THE UNIVERSE.

FIGURE OUT THE CODE AND YOU WILL POSSESS IT.

FIND TRUE NORTH AND YOU WILL FIND YOUR WAY HOME.

1. The first two numbers are the basis of the universe when separated but together they are a completion of a cycle.

2. The next two numbers are the antithesis of 1.

3. A hundred score will give you four numbers, but take away the sum of the first two pairs and you will get the last two pairs.

What a very cryptic riddle... and so remarkably intriguing. I enjoy puzzles. I've never heard of a dedication to someone like this but I guess it keeps things interesting. I grabbed onto the box. I tried to shake the box but it barely moved. I pushed on the top of it but it would not give in. This was definitely an unusual sight to see. I examined it more thoroughly and I could not see any crevices around the box. I wasn't sure how it would open. This box was secured pretty well. It appeared that figuring out the code seemed like the only way to open this box. After a minute, I decided I would come check this out again later. Maybe Laura knew something about it.

    I turned around and crossed the street again and got to the steps of the library. It was a very old stone building. It looked, strangely, almost colonial. I looked at the top of the building where it just said *Town Library* in stone. I would've found some humor in them calling it the Return Library.

    I entered the building and as the door closed behind me, I was caught in the awe of how large this place was. The library had a high ceiling supported with marble columns and the walls were stone. In the ceiling was also a large glass dome where the sunlight would pour into the building and reflect off the floor. The walls were complimented with a few stained glass windows letting in multi-colored rays of light. There were three stories with bookshelves. I did see a few people sitting at tables and reading.

    There was a marble statue of a man with a long coat and long hair holding a couple books in his left hand and an old pistol in his right. The visage on his face looked like determination. He seemed like someone who fought for what he believed in. The statue appeared old but the detail on the face was quite remarkable. Strangely enough, his face sort of looked familiar but I couldn't place it.

RICHIE LEYLAND

The plaque below the statue read:

This Library is dedicated to Jeffrey Fitzgerald Hammond. Founder, Scholar, Teacher, Humanitarian, Friend.

Everyone deserves the opportunity to better themselves and has the divine right to exercise their freedoms and liberties without oppression by any form of government, whether legitimate or corrupt.
- Jeffrey Fitzgerald Hammond
(From his inaugural speech as the First Mayor of Return.)

Wow, this guy must have done something incredible.
I looked over and saw the History section. I immediately noticed a book on Jeffrey Fitzgerald Hammond. I pulled the book from the shelf and looked at the cover. There was Hammond's face and I couldn't shake the familiar feeling that I've seen his face before but I've never heard of the guy. I flipped the book around and looked at the back.

It gave a brief summary of how he organized a group of scholars to take back the town from a group of criminals and corrupt local government officials. When the people took back the town, it was acknowledged as a new town by the federal government and was renamed Return to symbolize the path it took to bring this town back to the people.

Wow.
I placed the book back on the shelf. I saw another section further down that just said Non-Fiction.
I guess History and Non-Fiction are separate?

RETURN

I walked on the path between the first two book cases and just randomly picked up the first book from the shelf. It was a small hard cover. I looked at the front. All it said was *First Day*. I searched the rest of the cover and there was nothing else. No author, no summary, nothing.

I opened up the book and read from the first page.

The light was blinding. I was lost. My lungs opened and burned with oxygen. I cried out in fear but I was also overwhelmed with euphoria.

I closed the book. That was a bit strange. I put the book back. I walked along the case some more and found another book.

The Funeral.

No author and no summary on this book as well. I opened the book to a random page and read an excerpt.

I stood in front of the casket as the woman in the black dress and black veil held my hand. My whole world had changed in the blink of an eye and I was swallowed by confusion, sadness, and anger within that moment.

At that moment, I decided that I didn't feel like being sad. I had enough emotions going through me currently. I put that one back. I picked up another book that was titled *When I Decided I No Longer Wanted to Play Football*. Again, no author and no summary.

I opened up the book in the middle and began

reading a sentence.

I was handed the ball and started to run around one of my guards but I missed it when one of their defensemen charged into me from below and I felt my ribs crack.

Ah, shit. I know how that goes.
I experienced a very similar injury in high school and I haven't played football in years. Some people just have the talent and the skill and I wasn't cut out for it. I wasn't in the mood for this book either; I put the book back. I kept walking along and found a book called *Graduation*, which sounded boring but it looked just like the other books. No author and no summary. I kept walking. There was another one titled *Perfect Date* and that also had no author and no summary. I didn't feel like reading Romance.

I walked to the end of the aisle and found a book on the end of the top shelf titled *The Catalyst*. Interesting title and no author and no summary. I opened up the book to a random page and read the first paragraph I saw:

"Why were you hanging out with him?!", he said. He was passionate for her but she lost patience with him. "I could ask the same about you! Why were you with her?", she asked.

"I told you that I've never seen that woman before in my life! I don't know where the hell those are coming from but I swear that is not me in those pictures! Why won't you believe me?! I wouldn't ever do that to you!"

He pleaded with her and he was not understanding why

she wouldn't believe him.
"Well, I wouldn't do that to you either."
"He's your ex-boyfriend and he doesn't like me. He's such a lying and cheating piece of shit! He's willing to say whatever or do whatever in order to get you back, Heidi!", he said. "You don't know him, Charlie!", she protested.

WHAT. THE. FUCK.
I looked around and saw everyone currently paying attention to what they were reading. Nobody was looking at me but I felt so uncomfortable reading this that I felt like I was being watched.
I heard the front door open. I looked at those paragraphs and read them again.
I read that correctly. This is the fight we had. This can't be a coincidence.
What is going on? Where the hell am I?
"Charlie..."
I closed the book, put it back on the top shelf and turned around.
Laura was standing there looking happy to see me and I was not expecting her to look like that.

SIX

Laura was standing in front of me with her beautiful flowing auburn hair down instead of up in a bun. She was wearing a red and white button-down plaid shirt with the top button open that was slightly exposing the cleavage of her firm breasts. Her shirt was tucked into a pair of blue jeans that contoured perfectly to her toned body. She had a belt with a big oval shaped bronze buckle around her waist holding up those jeans and she dressed them over her Western boots.

She dressed just like Heidi at the Halloween party last week but without the hat. At the party, we were playing cowboy and cowgirl and both of us loved it. It ignited a spark between us that we had not felt in quite a long time. We had incredible sex that night and it finally seemed that our relationship was getting back on track. Both of us were going through a rough patch recently and there were forces outside of our relationship that were contributing to it. We were so good and happy together throughout most of our relationship and we finally seemed to get back to creating that synergy at the Halloween party. It's quite unbelievable how quickly your life can change in 24 hours.

    I focused back on Laura.

    "Hey." I smiled at her. I was very happy to see her but sort of anxious too since I unintentionally became aroused. I tried to distract myself from it by asking questions.

    "How did you find me?", I asked her as I was trying to ease the activity in my loins.

    "Well, you brought up books earlier and I figure this would've been a good place to start." She put her hands in her pockets, leaned against the bookcase, crossed her feet and looked at me confidently, while gently biting her lip.

    Yeah, that didn't help. I felt my pants getting tighter.

    "Looks like you've been here for a while.", she said. I was somewhat perplexed by that statement. It didn't seem like I spent the whole day here.

    "Um, I don't think so. I haven't been in town very long."

    "Really? It's almost 4 o'clock. That's why I came looking for you."

    "4 o'clock? It couldn't have been that long."

    Laura looked at me like I was crazy and pointed in

the direction of the front door. The bookcase obscured my view so I started to move by her without being inappropriate and saw that she was pointing at an obnoxiously large clock above the door.

It was almost 4 o'clock.

"Wow, time flies when you're curious, I guess." I said to make light of the situation.

"C'mon, follow me. Time to get ready for dinner.", she instructed. As soon as she turned around, I immediately checked her out. Those Levi's were hugging that perfect ass of hers and they fit her like a glove. It was hypnotic as I was watching her walk away. I wanted her.

Stop it!
Stop staring at her ass!
Control yourself!
Be a gentleman, you fucking pig.

I snapped out of it and jumped a few extra paces to catch up with her.

As we walked out the front door, I saw that more stuff had been set up for the festival. There were now a few tents set up and in one of them, a stage had been erected.

Don't use that word.

"Oh, there's the mayor and his wife.", Laura said.

I looked around but I couldn't see who Laura was talking about. I looked back at her and she had a smile on her face as she looked across the other side of the town square and waved. I turned to look in that direction but then I saw the backs of the well dressed couple. He had on a gray suit and she wore a periwinkle blue dress. They entered the

Town Hall then the doors closed behind them.

"I'm sure you'll meet them at the festival. They're great people.", she said. "C'mon, let's go."

We descended the stairs and her red pickup was just to the right of us parked in the street. I was about to get in and I looked across the street and both of us noticed Tyler.

I went flaccid.

He was staring at us with that same dirty look he gave me the other day. I felt my blood pump more vigorously in my heart. I was getting annoyed with that dirty look. I stared back at him and he gave me the finger. This time, I chose to speak up about it.

I sternly asked him, "Hey, what's your deal? What did I do to you? Why can't you leave us alone?"

"It's a free town and a free country, *Charlie*.", responded Tyler.

I hated how he said my name.

"Which means I can stare as much as I want. I can do this, too."

Tyler flipped me the bird again.

"Charlie," said Laura. "Just ignore him. He doesn't put any effort into his relationships so don't put any effort into him."

"What did you say, bitch?", shouted Tyler. He stormed across the road and I ran over to get in front of him before he got to Laura. Tyler and I both grabbed each other in the middle of the street and then we heard a police siren. I looked to my right and there was a police car that pulled up and stopped in front of us. I let go of Tyler. Tyler didn't let go immediately but it finally hit him after a few seconds that maybe it was a good idea.

A policeman exited out of the car. He put on his hat and walked over to us. He was an older man with a slightly weathered face but looked younger than Henry.

"Now what are you two fellas, doing?", the Sheriff asked.

I stood there giving him the silent treatment. I think Tyler was just mimicking what I was doing. He seemed stupid enough to not know how to make toast.

"Hi, Sheriff.", said Laura.

"Laura, good to see you. How's your father?"

"He's good."

"Good. Maybe you can help me out here with what's going on?", asked Sheriff Carver.

"It's nothing, Sheriff. Just a misunderstanding. Right, guys?" She gave me a dead serious look. "Yes, sir. Just a misunderstanding.", I confirmed. I looked over at Tyler and I caught a brief glimpse of that dirty look he seemed to favor and then he nodded at the Sheriff.

The Sheriff then added, "Tyler, you are on probation. If I catch you starting more trouble, I will throw you in jail without hesitation. Are we clear?"

"Yes, Sheriff.", responded Tyler.

"Good, be on your way now.", said the Sheriff. Tyler walked away from us and continued down the street. The Sheriff then focused on me. "Well, I like to get acquainted with any new face that comes into town. What's your name, bud?"

"It's Charlie. Charlie Denton."

"Charlie. That's my father's name. Wonderful name. Sheriff Jack Carver. Pleased to meet you." He extended his hand. I reached for it and grabbed it perfectly with a solid grip.

"Nice handshake. That tells quite a bit about someone you know."

"Oh, yeah. What does that say about me?"

"Nothing criminal." He winked.

I chuckled and we withdrew our hands. "So Charlie, where are you staying? Are you at the hotel?", the sheriff asked.

"No, I'm sort of stranded in town right now and Laura has been so very kind for letting me crash at her place.", I answered back.

"Well, you got a bargain staying with her. She's a great cook. It's beautiful out that way and you have a beautiful view of the lake. Go check out the lighthouse. You won't regret it.", he suggested.

"Thank you, Sheriff. I might just do that."

"Charlie... Laura... you kids stay out of trouble."

"Thanks, Sheriff.", both of us simultaneously said. He got back into his car and we walked back to the truck. The police car kept on advancing down the road.

We got in the truck. She started up the engine and zoomed out of her parking spot with a subtle ferocity. She seemed very annoyed running into Tyler. She turned on to a road that cut through the middle of the town square. She then circled around the other sides of the block in the middle of the square and turned back on to the road to the farm. The trip seemed to be unusually fast as we were back at her house in what seemed to be seconds. She was probably hauling ass in the truck and I did not notice until we got to her road.

We got out of the truck and she walked towards her house. "I'm going to start preparing dinner.", she told me.

"Sounds good. Do you need any help?", I asked.

"No, but thank you. I got it."

"Okay, well, I'm going to stay outside then.", I said.

"Sweetie?", said Henry. I looked over to the right and there he was, covered in dirt and sweat in his cowboy attire.

"Hi, Dad. What's up?"

"Jack just called me. What did Tyler do?", asked Henry. Laura sighed.

"Dad, it's nothing. It was just Tyler being Tyler."

"Oh, so you mean he was an asshole?", quipped Henry.

I laughed out loud and Henry looked at me with an intense look but I saw him trying to hide a smirk forming on his face.

"Yeah, he was. He got angry and Charlie stopped him from getting near me."

"That's what Jack told me."

Henry walked over to me and extended his hand. I grabbed his hand firmly. Another great shake.

"Jack also said you had a good handshake." He withdrew his hand. "I appreciate what you did for my daughter. Tyler is an asshole. Don't associate with him."

"It's not a problem. I agree with you.", I reassured

him. I saw a smirk slowly form on the edge of his mouth.

Henry turned around and walked towards the house. "I'm done for the day. I gotta shower. I smell like shit. Please let me know when dinner is ready.", he said. Laura opened the door. Henry entered and Laura followed behind him as the door closed.

I think I may have just got through the big man's armor and I think he realized it, too. It made me want Laura even more. After knowing her for only four days, I was falling for her very hard. I looked up at the sky and was mesmerized by how clear it was and the amount of different shades of blue that it exhibited. I couldn't believe how warm it was for early November. Jack was right. It really was beautiful out here. This town was unlike any place I've ever been and it was starting to grow on me.

I drifted away in my thoughts. I was looking out the window at the snow falling.

"Charlie?"

I turned around and saw my mother had called me. She was standing next to our Christmas tree holding a small box.

"Aren't you going to open your present?", she asked.

I looked down at my outfit. I was wearing a navy blue sweater along with a pair of khakis. *I'm a kid again.*

I remember this. This is the last Christmas I had with Mom and Dad. I saw my father enter the room and Uncle Greg was right behind him.

"Go ahead, my boy. Open it up.", said my father.

Uncle Greg walked up to our sofa and parked himself on an end.

"Come on, pal. Have a seat next to me. I want to see what you got.", Uncle Greg said.

I walked over to my mother and took the small box from her. I saw that this was from Uncle Greg. My uncle patted the cushion next to him on the sofa and I sat in that position. My father sat down next to me on the other side.

I tore the wrapping paper off of the box and now I remember this.

The compass. I haven't used it in so long.

I opened the box and the brand new compass was inside the box.

"This is so cool! Thanks, Uncle Greg!"

"You're very welcome, Charlie!", he said to me.

"I know you've been wanting to go camping for a long while so we will go soon when the weather gets nicer.", my dad told me.

My parents' accident happened shortly after I got this compass. We never went camping. I am grateful that Uncle Greg eventually taught me how to use the compass.

"I will show how to you use the compass later. This is a very valuable tool to have when you are out in the wilderness. Just remember if you're ever lost, as long as you find true north, you will find your way home.", my father explained.

"Thanks, Dad." I hugged him.

I heard a faint ringing of a bell that was gradually and relentlessly making its presence known. The ringing became

RETURN

overwhelming and pulled me away from my memory.

SEVEN

I woke up. I was laying in a field just relaxing and the picture perfect clear sky was all I saw in my peripheral view. Laura was ringing a dinner bell. "Ready!", she hollered. I found that amusing since I've never been summoned by a dinner bell before. I got up from the grass. I walked over to the house and entered through the front door. As soon as I stepped inside, that heavenly scent of steak slapped me in the face. I was salivating at the thought of it. I walked over to the dining room table and Laura pointed at a plate.

"You're there.", she said. I saw an enormous cut of meat occupying half of the plate in front of me, accompanied by a giant scoop of mashed potatoes and green beans.

"Oh, wow. This looks and smells incredible.", I said.

"Thanks.", she replied back. "Please... sit."

I sat down, admiring the gorgeous creation in front of me and then Henry walked in and sat down next to me. "It smells great, Sweetie.", he said. "Thank you, Dad.", as she accepted the compliment. Laura sat down and grabbed my right hand then she grabbed Henry's left hand and Henry grabbed my left hand. They bowed their heads and I followed suit.

Henry began in prayer.

"Dear Lord, thank you for this meal we are about to enjoy, the shelter we have, and for looking out for our family and friends, old... and new."

I smiled.

"Amen", he concluded.

"Amen", Laura and I said in unison.

That was a nice prayer. It felt comforting to hear.

Usually, I do not have sentiments like that regarding prayer. I'm not much of a religious person. It's sort of hard to be when God takes away your parents and you're a child left abandoned with no explanation. I hated it whenever someone would say 'God works in mysterious ways.' It's such a bullshit platitude.

"Alright, let's dig in.", said Henry.

I cut into the steak and it was cooked just how I liked it, medium rare. I bit into it and it was carnivorous bliss.

"Oh... the steak is perfect. Just stellar.", I praised.

"Yeah, she cooks just as good as her mother.", Henry added.

"So I'm told.", Laura cheerfully acknowledged.

"So Charlie, how about your parents?", asked Henry. I saw Laura give a look of warning to Henry and she slightly shook her head.

"What? What did I say?", Henry inquired.

"It's okay. Um, I lost both my parents a long time ago when I was very young. I was 12."

Henry looked down at his plate and I could see he momentarily felt bad about that. I kept cutting pieces of my steak off just to ease the immediate stress I felt.

"Charlie, I'm... I'm sorry. That couldn't have been easy.", Henry sympathized. He then added, "Do you mind me asking how they died?"

"Dad, stop...", Laura interjected.

"No, it's okay. I don't mind.", I responded.

Actually, I didn't mind. I felt comfortable around the both of them.

"My parents went on a cruise for their 20th anniversary. My Uncle Greg watched me while they were on their vacation. The cruise ship was just off the southern tip of Florida and one of the engines exploded. It caused massive damage to the hull and the ship sank. Some people made it off the ship but my parents did not."

I looked over at Laura and her mouth was slightly agape. I could tell she was sympathetic but also understood what I went through. She did lose her mother after all when she was a teenager.

"I guess I have to thank them for my education. I was part of a class action lawsuit against the cruise company and we won. I was rewarded enough to get me through school and start my own life.", I added. I took another bite and swallowed. "I liked playing football when I was young. I thought it would've been cool to have a scholarship playing ball and maybe play in the NFL someday but I wasn't cut out for it." I went back to eating my meal.

"You used to play football?", Henry asked. I could see he wanted to quickly change the topic.

"Yeah, I did!"

"Me too."

"Oh yeah, what position did you play?"

"Fullback."

He looked it, that's for sure. "Cool. I was a Wide Receiver. After I got injured in high school, I decided it wasn't for me and I took a different route in life." I looked at Henry. "When did you play?", I asked.

"I played ball for the Army. Army paid for my education, too. I had a career in the Army for quite awhile. I've fought on the ground but I eventually became a pilot and I spent a significant portion of my military career flying."

"That's amazing. I've always thought that flying various aircraft would be a great skill to have."

I wasn't lying. I continued with my meal.

He looked over at Laura. "Well, I'm sure she could give you a lesson." I looked at her, pleasantly surprised.

"You know how to fly?", I asked.

"He taught me when I was young, actually when Mom was still alive. I've flown planes and I've even flown that blimp that you saw in the middle of town today.", Laura said.

"That thing is so old.", said Henry. He took a bite of his steak.

"It's in better shape than you think.", Laura rebutted. Henry swallowed his bite hard.

"You better check it out before the festival starts. You don't have much time.", added Henry.

"Oh it'll be fine. I'll be there tomorrow all day looking at it to make sure it is in good shape. Nothing a little perseverance and duct tape can't fix.", Laura said.

"Pfft, duct tape...", Henry said with a tone of apathy. He put another piece of steak in his mouth.

After Henry threw in the final word, I finished the last of my green beans and mashed potatoes. I only had a few bites of steak left. I woofed that steak down. *I must've been very hungry.* I finished off my last few bites and set the fork and knife on the plate.

"That was incredible, Laura. That might've been the best steak I've ever had in my life. Thank you.", I said. She finished her last piece too and smiled at me as she wiped her mouth clean. I looked at Henry and he was devouring the last piece he had. He laid back in his chair and satisfyingly held his stomach. "Thank you, Sweetie.", Henry said. "Both of you are very welcome.", she responded. She collected our plates and utensils then walked into the kitchen.

I looked outside and noticed that the sun just went down. Henry turned to me and asked, "So what's going on with you tonight?" One particular thought did cross my mind.

"Well", I started. "Jack mentioned I should go check out the lighthouse. He said I wouldn't regret it."

"That's a good idea. You should. The view is beautiful and the lighthouse is quite a piece of history."

"What's so significant about the lighthouse?", I asked. Henry sat back up in his chair.

Henry answered, "Jeffrey Fitzgerald Hammond used the lighthouse as a secret place for the scholars who partook in the town revolution. Below the lighthouse is a secret meeting room where they would discuss their plans to overthrow the town and take it back for the people. Hammond also used the lighthouse as a way to signal to ships from nearby neighboring towns throughout the New England states. Lots of outsiders heard of the corrupt local government operating here and for a new country in its infancy and what the people had to do to get their freedom, they organized and took down the corrupt local government."

"Wow. Everything I've heard about this guy is just extraordinary. I've never heard of him before either. Why didn't they teach about him in when I was in school?", I asked.

"Well Charlie, winners of wars get to write history but whoever is in power gets to choose what's printed.", said Henry. He stood up from his chair and looked down on me. He put his hand on my shoulder and it felt like a catcher's mitt.

"I'm going to call it a night shortly but you two have fun.", he said. Then his grip tightened slightly on my shoulder and he got close to my ear. "Charlie, I like you and I can tell Laura really likes you too. I just want to remind you that there will be no hot and heavy stuff going on in my house tonight. Clear?"

"Crystal.", I replied.

"Good."

He let go of my shoulder. He walked into the kitchen and I could hear them chat quickly but I couldn't make it out. I got up and walked into the kitchen. As I entered, I saw that Laura was finishing up the dishes. Henry patted her gently on her shoulder and kissed her on the cheek. "Good night, sweetie.", he said.

"Good night, Dad.", she said back. He then looked at me and walked on past me.

"Night, Charlie."

"Night, Henry."

I heard him climb the stairs and the heavy footsteps faded away. Laura was drying off her hands with a towel. She placed the towel down on the counter next to the sink and looked at me. "What are you planning on doing this evening?"

Then I had a good idea.

I asked, "Would you like to come with me to the lighthouse?" She smiled and then said "Sure. It's a date."

EIGHT

I was sitting in one of the rocking chairs outside on the front porch waiting for my hot date. I was admiring the stars that were slowly coming through as the sky darkened. The sound of Laura's boots were approaching the door then she walked out and closed the door behind her. I stood up from the rocking chair. I looked at her and noticed she put on some lipstick, the shade was slightly darker than the color of her lips, and a little mascara. I didn't think she needed it.
She's beautiful even without the makeup.
"Ready to go?", I asked.
"Let's do it.", she complied.

Don't think about innuendos.

We walked off of her front porch towards the road and headed in the direction of the lighthouse. We reached the end of the road and the pavement slowly transformed into grass. We were treading through the long grass and I took notice of the moon. It seemed unusually large but it was lighting up our whole way very well so I wasn't complaining.

"The moon is large tonight.", she said.

"Hah, I was just thinking that. I don't think I've seen it that big before."

"I have, but then again, when you have been living in a small town your whole life, I guess anything outside of it could seem big."

Interesting perspective.

"You've lived here your whole life?", I asked.

"Yep. Born and raised. I love it here. I'm a small town country girl through and through. How about you? Where are you living?"

"Well, I live back in Buffalo. Just outside of the city. I've lived there most of my life."

"Do you like living out there?", she asked.

"Yeah. I'm not far away from some of my family which is nice. I'm just accustomed to it, I suppose.", I replied.

"I understand that. Sometimes family is all we have."

Ain't that the truth.

We were nearing the lighthouse and it was taller than I anticipated. I also realized it was on the edge of a cliff and the lake was below us. The lighthouse was covered in a coat of ivory with a stone foundation and the light was spinning.

I walked up to the steel door entrance and held it open for her.
    "After you.", I said.
    "Thank you." She smiled.
    She entered, I walked in behind her and the door closed behind us. I looked to my right and saw a donation box for the lighthouse. Laura reached into her pocket and pulled two one dollar bills out of her pocket. She dropped them into the open slot on the top of the donation box. I also saw a staircase to our left that went upstairs and a door in front of us that was open. Laura pointed at the doorway in front of us.
    "Let's go through that door first.", she suggested.
    "Sounds good to me.", I agreed.
    We walked through the open doorway and descended a flight of stairs. When we got down to the bottom, we both noticed a painting of Jeffrey Fitzgerald Hammond hanging on the wall in front of us. Laura stopped and looked at it then looked at me.
    "Huh. I didn't realize it before, but you kind of look like him.", Laura stated then began to walk down the short hallway on our right.
    "Really?"
    Maybe that's why he looked familiar. I'm a doppelgänger.
    "If you say so...", I concluded. Laura rounded a corner and I followed her. Around it, we found an open room that looked like a study and the walls were lined with bookcases containing very old books and manuscripts. There were banisters and railings blocking the bookcases around

the walls, probably to keep people from touching these books. In the middle of the room was a small square table blocked off with four stanchions on the corners that were connected to each other with a velvet rope. There was sign that was in front of the table that read:

This is where Jeffrey Fitzgerald Hammond and his allies planned out the uprising to take back the town of Return.

I've always found things like this in history to be quite remarkable. It's also kind of strange how inanimate objects maintain a significance due to a historical event.
"Wow.", I said.
"Yeah, it's quite something. It was incredible how much he fought for the citizens in this town.", Laura added.
I looked back at the bookcases and noticed another sign in front of the one of the bannisters. This one read:

Jeffrey Fitzgerald Hammond's personal library and book collection.

I looked at it again and realized there were probably a couple thousand books organized along these walls.
"Incredible. I would love to look at these books.", I said.
"Me too. Unfortunately, these books are too fragile for anyone to look at.", Laura said.
"Yeah, I figured. Wow, there's just so much knowledge here." I was just in awe and admiring Hammond's will to collect all these books.
"A personal library? Did he live here?", I asked.

"Not in the lighthouse. He lived on this land in a small cabin, very close by.", Laura answered.

"He probably couldn't fit all these books in there.", I joked. She smiled. I kept looking along the walls and noticed one part of a wall where there wasn't a bookcase; instead there was a painting. It looked like a circle, no... more like an ellipse formed out of boulders and below the ellipse was a horizontal line also made up of boulders. The outer edges of the painting were covered with trees. Below the painting was a name plate that said:

The Beginning and The End.

"That's an interesting painting.", I commented.

"That is not far from the farm.", Laura added. I was surprised by the response and I turned to looked at her. "You mean that actually exists?", I asked.

"Yep, it's in the woods just near our property.", she confirmed.

Bizarre.

"Okay, so follow me. Let me show you the top of the lighthouse.", said Laura. She started to walk down the hallway and back up the stairs as I followed her. When she was nearing the top she was climbing every stair slowly and I was distracted by her perfect ass in those Levi's. When she got to the last stair, she stopped and I bumped into her. I heard her giggle and she climbed the last stair back on to the ground floor. When I got up to the floor, she turned around with a big smile and playfully scratched at my chest. She

then spun forward and kept walking ahead of me.
She did that on purpose. Henry was right.
"Come on. We got a few floors to climb.", she said.
She grabbed my hand and we started climbing the stairs. Fortunately, we were both fit enough that the four flights of stairs were a breeze. We got to the top floor. Laura climbed the ladder and I followed her upward. She knew where she was going plus I liked what I saw as I was looking up.
Dammit, man. Cut it out.
She reached the top of the ladder which led to a hatch in the ceiling. Laura opened the hatch and we climbed through the opening. We were on a balcony and the light was still spinning a few feet above us. I looked out at the view and it was magnificent. It was an endless horizon of sky and water.
"Wow.", I said.
"Yeah, that's the easiest thing to say.", she said.
I smiled wide at her and she smiled back. I thought about it and I realized that I felt okay right now. I was near the water and I was relaxed.
"Actually," I started, "this is very nice. Thank you for coming with me. This is sort of a big deal for me."
Laura curiously looked at me with a smile on her face. "Why is this a big deal for you?", she genuinely asked. She walked a couple steps closer to me without breaking eye contact.
I reluctantly looked at her.
"It's okay. I won't judge you.", she reassured me.
"I... haven't been comfortable around water for a long

time... since from when my parents died. This is the first time since then where I do not feel... an uneasy sensation in the pit of my stomach. And by 'water', I mean more like ponds, lakes, and oceans. I can deal with baths, pools, and puddles.", I confessed.

Laura had the oddest look on her face. I couldn't tell if she was trying to be empathetic or if she was trying to laugh.

Oh no. I broke her. :-D

"Charlie..."

She gently grabbed my face and gave me a slow tender kiss on the lips. *Holy shit. She just kissed me.*

"I am glad that you feel this relaxed right now and if I can help you in any way in dealing with this, please let me know.", she responded.

"Thank you, Laura.", I said with sincerity.

I looked at the horizon again and then looked back at her.

"The kiss was pretty great, too.", I added. *Yep, I just said that and she just laughed.* I looked into her eyes and I kissed her back. I earned it. We held each other and connected our lips. I loved how she tasted. We slowly kissed for a few seconds and then let go. We kept holding each other. I turned to her side, put my arm around her and looked at the horizon with her. She leaned into me.

Everything felt right at this very moment. I don't know what it was but I felt completely at ease. This date was going well and I didn't have a care in the world. An extremely beautiful woman just kissed me and I kissed her

back. I felt no awkwardness despite my situation of losing my long time girlfriend and being stranded in a town that I never even knew existed. For circumstances like these, this would be a complicated and stressful situation for anyone but I couldn't explain why in this moment I felt pretty great. So, I decided to not think about it and enjoy this as much as I could. We stood there for a few more minutes just admiring the view and keeping each other warm. I was happy just holding on to her.
    Ow.
    I reached at my head.
    "Are you OK?", she asked.
    "Yeah... my head just hurts a little.", I said.
    "Okay, date's over. Let's go. You should be getting rest.", she commanded.
    "Yeah, you're right. Let's go.", I agreed.
    We descended the ladder and closed the hatch behind us. We got down the stairs safely and departed the lighthouse. My head wasn't hurting so much anymore but better safe than sorry. *I'm not a nurse. I'll listen to the nurse.*
    We walked back to the farm and we held hands. She started humming "Everlong" by the Foo Fighters.
    I love that song.
    I looked at her with a smile on my face and started humming along with her. She grabbed my hand and we continued with the melody. We headed back to the farm and hummed the whole song up until the end. We got to the side of the barn where the guest room was then I opened the door and stepped inside. She stayed outside. I turned

around and looked into those beautiful eyes.

"Is there anything else you'd like before you go to sleep?", she asked.

I was thinking of her.
I'd like her before I go to sleep.
Stop it. You're not thinking clearly right now.
"No, I think I'm alright.", I replied.

"Okay. I'll be leaving early tomorrow morning to go into town to help with setting up the festival. Just so you know where I am. Henry might be around though. I know he will take it easy from now up until next Monday. It's one of the very few times of the year where he takes a small break from working.", she said.

"Thanks, I'll probably just go into town and see what's going on whenever I get up. I'll come find you.", I said.

"Sounds good.", she agreed.

She grabbed my shirt and pulled me toward her. She kissed me then slipped me a little tongue and then she let me go.

"Good night, Handsome.", she said.
"Good night, Gorgeous.", I said back.

She looked at me with a wide smile and started to walk back to the house. She turned around to look at me one more time with a smile then faced forward and kept on walking. I stepped back and closed the door. I went into the bedroom and stripped off my clothes. I collapsed onto the bed and felt pretty good about our date. It relaxed me so well that I was able to drift into sleep easier than a narcoleptic that ingested an entire bottle of cough medicine.

RETURN

NINE

    I woke up. I saw the newspaper on the nightstand and picked it up. I opened it up and looked at the date. Thursday, November 7th.
    Good. I'm glad that I didn't sleep for another three days.
    I looked over to my left and saw a couple more T-shirts, a couple pairs of socks and another pair of jeans sitting on the chair. I also saw a tray on top of the dresser. It had a glass of orange juice and a plate covered with a chrome top. I walked over to the dresser and uncovered the plate. There were some scrambled eggs, three pieces of bacon, two slices of wheat toast and a few strawberries.
    She's awesome. I swear she must have a sixth sense when

it comes to food I like.
    I noticed a note laying underneath the knife and fork. I picked it up and it read:

> Good morning. I made you breakfast.
> I'll be in the town square for most of the day.
> Call me or come see me if you need anything.
> 716-525-4365.
> XOXO,
> Laura.

    I put the note down on the counter and started on breakfast. It was lukewarm but still very good. I looked at the clock and saw that it was just past 10. I finished my breakfast.
    Even with my breakfast semi-cold, Laura is such a good cook.
    I put on my clothes from yesterday and picked up the tray along with a T-shirt. I went outside and walked towards the house. It was another sunny and warm November day. Henry was walking along the crops in the fields. He waved at me and I waved back. I entered the house with the tray and set it on the kitchen counter. I went into the bathroom, did my business then took a shower. The water was soft and it was refreshing. It hit me that I hadn't showered since I got to the farm.
    Gross. Laura must really like me.
    I stepped out of the shower and pulled a towel out of the closet in the bathroom. I dried myself off and got dressed. I left the bathroom then walked over to the laundry

room and dropped the towel into the hamper. On my way out the front door, I noticed a photograph hanging on the wall. It was a picture of a younger Henry along with another woman with auburn hair, which I figured had to be Laura's mom and a little girl also with auburn hair, which I figured had to be Laura. Everyone in the picture had the biggest smile and they were caught in a loving embrace with each other. It made me think of my parents.
I miss that feeling.
When I was done admiring the photo, I walked outside and saw Henry loading lumber into the back of a blue pickup truck in front of the open garage. He noticed me coming out of the house. I started walking toward him.

"Good morning, Charlie.", he said.

"Good morning, Henry."

"You mind giving me a hand?", he asked.

"No, not at all."

He loaded the last plank in his arms into the back of the truck and we both walked into the garage. There was a pile of lumber sitting in the middle of it.

"Here," as he pointed to the left side of the pile, "take these ones."

I grabbed a few planks from the pile and tucked them under my right arm. I walked over to the truck and started loading them just like how Henry had started. Henry walked back to the truck with more lumber in his arms. I went back and grabbed more planks from the pile.

"How's your head?", he asked.

"It's okay. I'm not hurting right now.", I replied.

"Good, good."

I grabbed more planks and walked back to the truck. Henry loaded up his share and went back to the pile.

"What are the planks for?", I asked.

"I bring the lumber into town every year for any person that might need it for the festival. There are always various stands around during the festival, usually for food.", he explained.

"How much are we bringing?"

"We're bringing all of these size planks on the left side of the pile and whatever is in the back of the truck now.", he said.

We worked on that pile for a little bit longer and as soon as the back of the truck was nearly full, I put in one more plank. Henry said, "That's good." He closed the gate on the truck.

"I'm going to take this load into town now. Want a ride?", Henry asked.

"Sure.", I said.

Henry closed the garage and we both hopped in the truck. Henry started up this blue beast of a truck then proceeded out of the driveway and towards town. Henry turned on the radio and Led Zeppelin was playing. He started humming along and then I joined in.

This family has great taste in music.

We were in the town square within a flash. As we entered the square, Henry found a spot nearby and parked his truck along the inner side of the town square then turned the engine off. We both stepped out of the truck; we walked to the back of the truck and Henry opened the gate.

"Hey, gentlemen."

I turned around and saw Laura walking towards us. She was wearing a red t-shirt tucked into those jeans with her big buckle and her boots. She was also sporting a navy blue baseball cap and her hair was in a ponytail that was pulled through the hole in the back.

"Hi there.", I happily said to her.

"Hey, sweetie.", said Henry.

"How's your head today, Charlie?", Laura asked.

"It's alright. I'm feeling better.", I said.

"Great.", she said and smiled. She then added, "Don't worry about this. We can get people to help unload this if necessary. What I would like you to do is go get lunch. I just put a call into Martha's for some sandwiches for the three of us. I ordered you a turkey with cheese, lettuce, tomato and mayo. Is that okay?"

"That's perfect. Thanks.", I replied.

"No problem. Here's some cash; it should be enough." She handed me a twenty dollar bill.

"Dad, I ordered you a ham and cheese on wheat.", Laura added.

"Thank you, sweetie.", said Henry. He took a few planks out of the truck and Laura and I both stepped away from the truck to give him room. He started carrying them to the center of the square. Laura looked back at me.

"Martha said it should be ready in about 15 minutes. Do you remember how to get there?"

I did remember.

"Yeah, I should manage." I said with a grin on my face.

"Alrighty, see you when you get back." She smiled at me and blew me a kiss. My smile got wider. I turned around and headed in the direction towards Martha's.

I passed by the iron box with the dials and took a glance.

Oh, I'll eventually figure you out, you strange metallic bastard.

I turned my head towards my destination and noticed the library as I was strolling by.

I have to go back there and I keep getting distracted.

Nonetheless, I kept on walking towards the diner.

I was approaching the end of the sidewalk and looked to my left above the town hall at the clock. It was a little bit after 1 o'clock. Time seemed to move fast in this town. I stopped at the corner of the intersection as traffic was slow but moving steady. I pressed the button on the traffic post and the signal across the street changed to inform me that it was okay to cross.

After I made my way across the street, I kept moving toward the diner then a downward slope began on the sidewalk. I was looking at the various shops; there was a barbershop across the street, a florist to the left of the barbershop and a pharmacy next to the florist. I turned my focus back to ahead of me and saw Martha's diner coming up.

As I neared the diner, I peered in and saw that the place was packed for lunch. Soup sounded good right now. I walked in and up to the counter then Martha immediately noticed me.

"Charlie! How are ya, Darlin'?", Martha asked.

"I'm better. Thanks, Martha.", I responded.

"Good! You look better.", she cheerfully said. "How can I help you, Charlie?"

"Laura placed a lunch order. I'm here to pick it up."

"I got it right here.", she said. She turned around and pulled a white paper bag off the counter behind her then placed the bag in front of me. She started punching numbers into the register.

"That'll be $18.96.", Martha said.

I handed her the twenty dollar bill.

"Keep it.", I said.

"Thank you, Darlin'. Your business is appreciated. Tell Laura I say 'Hi.' Henry too, if you see him."

"Will do. Take care, Martha."

"You do the same, Charlie."

I picked up the bag and left the diner. I started heading back towards the town square and noticed a police car to my left slowing down. The person behind the wheel looked familiar.

"Hey, Charlie!", Jack called out.

"Hey, Sheriff!"

"Would you like a ride?", he asked.

"Sure, that'd be great.", I accepted. *This place is very welcoming.*

I got into the front passenger side of the police car and put on my seat belt. Jack began to drive.

"So what's going on today?," he asked.

"Just picking up lunch for Laura, Henry, and me.

Laura and Henry are helping out with setting up the festival.", I answered.

"Very nice. I love Martha's sandwiches. She's a culinary master.", Jack added.

"She won me over with her chicken noodle soup.", I said. Jack laughed and said, "Same here. Come to think of it, everything I've ever had from there is excellent. She makes an outstanding beef brisket."

He pulled up next to Henry's truck and put the police cruiser in park. I got out of the car and closed the door behind me.

"Thanks, Sheriff.", I said politely.

"You're welcome, Charlie."

Laura and Henry were both coming toward me. I handed the bag to Laura and Laura acknowledged the Sheriff.

"Hey, Sheriff.", she said.

"Laura. Henry.", addressed Jack.

"Jack.", Henry acknowledged and waved at him.

The Sheriff started driving again and continued down the road. I turned to Laura and she set the bag on the open gate of the truck. Most of the lumber had been unloaded out of the truck.

"Martha says 'Hi' to both of you.", I told them. Laura opened the bag and examined the order.

"She's so sweet.", spoke Laura.

She pulled our sandwiches out of the bag and distributed them to us. I unwrapped my sandwich and took a bite.

Jack was right. This sandwich is awesome.

RETURN

    I devoured it without thinking twice. It's odd that I was eating the sandwich like this when it felt like I just ate breakfast not that long ago. It looked like Laura and Henry were hungry as wolves and they were thoroughly enjoying their sandwiches. I took a napkin out of the bag then wiped my mouth and threw it back in the bag along with the wrapper for my sandwich. Laura and Henry both ate their sandwiches so quickly like food was scarce. Laura collected both of their wrappers and put them in the bag. She crumbled up the bag, arched her arm and tossed the bag into a nearby trashcan.

    Henry grabbed a few more planks out of the back of the truck and went back to the center of the square with them. I saw a woman wearing a camouflage cap with long jet black hair coming down from the cap and a pink T-shirt tucked into her jeans that were held up with a studded belt coming towards Laura and me.

    "You're right. He's much cuter than Tyler.", she said. Laura laughed. Laura looked at me.

    "Charlie... this is my best friend, Michelle.", said Laura. She looked at Michelle then pointed at me. "This is Charlie."

    "Hi, nice to meet you.", I said. We shook hands and she had a firm grip. "Likewise, Charlie.", Michelle responded.

    A young bald man in jeans, a T-shirt and work boots came up to the three of us. He got close to Michelle and wrapped his arms around her from behind. They both smiled. "Hey, who's this guy?", he asked.

"Charlie, this is my husband, Derek.", Michelle said.

"Hey, nice to meet you.", Derek said. He reached out and we shook hands. *Also, another successful shake. I'm making friends fast in this town.*

"Same here, Derek.", I said. Derek looked at Michelle.

"Hun,", Derek began, "we should get back to it. We're burning daylight."

"Is there anything I can help you with?", I asked.

Laura looked at me and said, "I'm sure we'll find you something."

We walked towards the center of the town square. I started helping Michelle and Derek with the construction of some stands and the setting up of various tables and chairs. Laura walked over to the blimp and then I saw her appear in the gondola. I figured that she was probably inspecting it to make sure everything operated smoothly.

I continued with other miscellaneous work that Michelle and Derek needed from me. We were making good progress on setting everything up and I was enjoying the company of everyone present.

After we set up a few more stands, a few hours had passed. Derek made the call that we were done and he thanked me. Michelle and him began to clean up. I looked back at Laura and saw that she was still running her check on the blimp. I've been so busy helping Derek and Michelle that I hadn't talked to Laura in quite a bit. I figure I would go check on her to see if she needed any help.

I walked up to the blimp and entered the passenger cabin. The interior was not what I expected. It had a metal frame, a metal floor, and metal seats with leather padding. However, the lower half of the gondola from the floor to the windows had sleek wooden paneling which almost gave it the appearance of the inside of a boat. A boat that could fly. The chairs for the pilot and co-pilot were padded seats with vinyl upholstery. I saw Laura sitting in the pilot's chair checking her switches and gauges on the dashboard.

"Hey, there.", I announced.
"Hey, you.", she responded.
"Do you need any help?" I moved closer to her.
"No, I'm good. How about you?"
"I'm perfectly fine. So how's it looking?"
"Oh, she's right as rain. I'm not worried. I have this right here.", she said then pointed at a tool box next to her feet. She opened it up and there was a roll of duct tape inside. I let out a slight chuckle.

"You're the expert. If that's what is necessary to be prepared then I'm in no position to judge.", I told her.

She got up from her seat then walked over to me and hugged me. She whispered into my ear "Don't worry. I've done this before." She kissed me on the cheek right after she said that. I felt more reassured after that. She sat back down in the seat and went back to examining the controls. I exited the gondola.

I went around the rear of the blimp and observed the clock on the top of the town hall. It was just past 5 o'clock.

We did a pretty good job. A lot of stuff was set up. I saw Michelle and Derek finishing cleaning up their work space along with the other volunteers who lent a hand with setting up the stands. I walked back to the truck and saw Henry there leaning against it drinking a bottle of water.

"All done?", I asked Henry.

"Yep, just waiting on Laura.", he said. I turned around and Laura was walking towards us.

"Hey," she started, "I'm going to stick around here a little longer. I'm not done checking out the blimp. I shouldn't be too much longer. I'll be home in a little bit and we'll get going with dinner."

"Sounds good, sweetie.", acknowledged Henry.

Laura went over to Henry and gave him a kiss on the cheek. She then came over to me and kissed me on the cheek.

"See you both soon.", she said and then she walked back to the blimp. Henry looked at me and shrugged his shoulders.

He then asked me, "Wanna go grab a beer?"

When in Rome, do as the Romans do.

"Sure. Where are we going?", I asked Henry.

"I know just the place."

TEN

Henry pulled into the parking lot of Lenny's Brewing Pub and parked the truck. We got out and walked towards the pub. The sunlight was diminishing and dusk was advancing.

"This guy brews his own beer?", I asked.
"He uses my hops.", said Henry.
"You grow hops?", I asked Henry.
"Yep. Some fruits and vegetables too."

We walked up to the door. I grabbed it and opened the door for him.

"Thanks.", said Henry. He walked inside.
"No problem.", I said back. I followed him in.

There were only a few patrons around. It was a pretty

small crowd for a happy hour. We walked up to the bar and tried to signal the bartender. She came over to us with a bit of pep in her step.

"What can I get ya?", she cheerfully asked.

"House Lager.", Henry said.

"Same.", I uttered.

She grabbed a couple pints and had a smooth fill for both glasses. Only a little head on the top, and the rest, a crisp lager. Henry threw down a twenty dollar bill.

"Don't worry. It's on me.", he said.

"Thank you.", I politely said. The bartender brought our pints to us.

"Thank you, Caitlin.", Henry said. Caitlin handed a pint to Henry and she handed the other pint to me. She picked up the twenty dollar bill.

"Of course, Henry.", said Caitlin. She walked over to the register and opened it. She made change and brought it back to Henry. Henry threw down a couple singles.

"Thanks.", Caitlin happily said.

"Cheers.", I said and then I raised a glass to him. He touched my glass. *Henry's a classy guy.* We both took a sip of our beers. We walked over to a table in one of the corners of the dining room and sat down.

"How are you feeling? Your head okay?", asked Henry.

"Yeah, it's been fine today. Thanks.", I said.

"Good. How's the room?", he asked.

"Everything has been great, Henry. I truly appreciate you letting me stay at the farm.", I said.

I wasn't lying. I was grateful of everything him and

Laura have done for me. He took a gulp of beer and swallowed it like an aspirin. He set the glass down in front of him and looked at me.

"You're welcome, Charlie. I'd like to thank you for your help today. I appreciate it. I'm not as young as I used to be.", he said.

"Sure thing, Henry.", I said.

"I don't like burdening Laura with some of these things so it's nice to have another set of hands around."

"I'm sure she would do anything for you, Henry.", I told him.

"I know. It's just that she works so hard at what she does. Whether it's on the farm or at the hospital."

"Well she's a very determined and confident woman. I imagine a parent will always be concerned about their child but she knows how to handle herself. You raised her well and I like her a lot, Henry. By the way, you were right about what you told me after dinner.", I admitted to him.

"Of course, I was. I know my daughter. Since she's met you, she's had this glow about her that I haven't seen in a long time. I've noticed that this is the happiest I've seen Laura in a while.", he confessed. He continued on. "Like... before she was even dating..." and then Henry noticed something behind me and his face slowly turned to an expression of subtle fury. I turned around and the distraction captured my attention.

Tyler was at the other end of the room near a pool table in the corner. Some other guy was with him. If he was hanging out with Tyler, then he was probably an asshole, too.

"Ah, shit...", I said with a quiet annoyance.

"Hey," Henry said. I turned around and faced him. "Forget about that asshole. We're going to finish our beers, we are getting into my truck and we are going back to my farm. I have a bigger reason than you do to kick his ass but it is not worth it."

"Yeah, you're right.", I agreed.

"Hey, *Charlie*...", Tyler taunted.

What a prick.

That same prick was coming towards us. I could tell he was already half in the bag.

"What are you up to?", he said in a condescending manner. He slowly walked over to me and I looked at him intensely. I stood up.

"I was helping with setting up the festival and now Henry and I are enjoying a beer." I decided to be polite.

"Yeah, while moving in on my girl, right?", stated Tyler. He moved a foot toward me. I could smell booze on his breath. I wasn't liking this.

I retorted back. "Last I checked, she didn't belong to anyone. She's free to make her own decisions."

Tyler took another step towards me and put his right hand in one of the front pockets of his jacket.

"Tyler, if you start something, I will call the police again!", Caitlin announced from the bar. He looked at her and yelled, "Hey Caitlin! How about you stop talking and use that mouth of yours to suck my cock, you slut!"

Caitlin looked pissed after hearing Tyler's remark. I saw her grab a rotary phone sitting on the bar and dial a number. I assumed she was making good on her threat.

Tyler looked back at me then took another step towards me and was getting uncomfortably close to my face. *What is his problem?* I stepped backwards and stayed focused on him.

"What? You wanna kiss me?! Back the fuck up!", I shouted in anger.

He pulled out a switchblade and swiped at me. I just dodged it.

"Did you just try to cut me?!", I screamed at him.

"What the fuck, Tyler?!", yelled Henry. Henry stood up out of his chair.

Tyler swiped at Henry and also just missed him. Henry was pissed. He grabbed his pint glass and smashed it on Tyler's hand, knocking the switchblade out of his hand. A volcanic splash of beer erupted and the glass crashed to the floor. Tyler doubled back to the pool table shaking his hand then he picked up a pool cue. Tyler's friend stood up from leaning against the wall just watching the shit show.

Henry looked at Tyler's friend.

"Sit down or I'll kick your ass.", Henry calmly said. Tyler's friend went to go sit on a stool near the pool table.

"What is your deal, man?! I didn't do anything to you!", I yelled to Tyler. Tyler came at me violently swinging and I was moving away from him in whichever direction I could. I heard the other patrons starting a commotion as I was trying to keep tables between us to limit his reach. I was stepping backwards quickly to keep my eyes on Tyler and keep the distance between us. My eyes remained focus on the drunk asshole in front of me that as I was stepping backwards, I eventually hit the bar behind me. The obstacle got me to turn around and I saw the rotary phone that Caitlin used was sitting on the bar within arm's reach.

I picked the phone up off the bar and blocked the incoming blow of his next swing. He swung at me again and I ducked. He took another swing. I got the phone up in front of my face and the cue snapped in half from the impact of hitting the phone. Tyler was dumbfounded.

In that moment, I took the opportunity and smashed the base of the phone across his face as the collision with his jaw also produced a ding.

Two teeth flew out of his mouth and landed on the bar. He fell backwards on to a stool and ricocheted towards the floor. I looked at him and said, "It's for you." Then I dropped the phone on the floor next to him and it landed with a discordant and crashing ding.

"Hold it right there, Charlie."

I looked up. Jack was standing at the end of the bar. His hands were on his belt.

"Hi, Sheriff.", I nervously said.

Oh, shit. Be cool.

Henry quickly walked over to Jack to greet him.

"Jack."

"Henry, could you tell me what's going on?", the Sheriff inquired.

"Tyler has been drinking, and from the looks of it, he's probably had a lot. He came at us with a switchblade. I knocked the blade out of his hands. It's on the ground near that table." Henry pointed to our table and continued on. "Tyler then grabbed a cue and was swinging it at Charlie. Charlie then grabbed the phone and hit him in the face with it. It was completely self defense.", Henry finished.

"That's the truth. I saw it happen. Tyler also sexually harassed me in front of everyone.", Caitlin added.

"I saw it, too. That's what happened.", said a patron.

"Me, too.", chided another.

"Okay, okay.", barked Jack. "I will get each of your statements." Another cop, probably Jack's deputy, entered the room.

"Harris.", Jack called.

"Yes, Sheriff?", Harris answered.

"Cuff Tyler until we figure this all out. We're taking him to the station.", commanded Jack. Harris pulled out his cuffs, put Tyler's hands behind his back, and handcuffed Tyler. He picked Tyler up off the floor and Tyler stood dazed.

"Let's go, Tyler.", urged Harris. Tyler was moaning in pain and was bleeding out of his mouth. Harris escorted him out of the bar.

"Charlie, have a seat.", Jack insisted.

I sat down on the stool next to me. Jack looked at Caitlin. "Caitlin, give him a water.", added Jack. I didn't want it but I accepted it anyway. Caitlin set the glass in front of me and I downed half of it. Jack walked over to the patrons and started talking with them. Caitlin moved around the bar and joined the patrons and Jack. He seemed to be confirming the story. I knew I wasn't at fault but I was still nervous.

I saw Deputy Harris walk back into the bar with a camera. He took the lens cap off the camera and started taking pictures of the area near our table and the pool table.

Henry walked over to me and grabbed some napkins from a dispenser on the bar. He was trying to clean some of the beer that splashed off of his sleeve then he threw them back on the bar. He put his hand on my right shoulder.

"Don't worry about this. Jack and I go way back. It's not your fault. I will vouch for you.", he reassured me.

"Thank you. I didn't want this to happen.", I said.

"I know you didn't.", Henry said.

"What about Laura?", I asked.

"I'll tell her the truth. She cares about you.", Henry said.

"I've never hurt someone like that before.", I confessed.

"What happened here doesn't give me a negative view of you. Okay?", said Henry.

I nodded at him and felt a great weight lift off of me. I saw Jack come back towards us. "Okay, they're telling me the same thing so I think you'll be fine, Charlie. I still need the both of you to come down to the station and give your statements."

Both Henry and I agreed and I stood up off the stool. Deputy Harris made his way over to the bar and took pictures of the rotary phone next to a small pool of Tyler's blood. We walked out of the pub and hopped in Henry's truck. We followed the Sheriff back to the police station.

My head started to hurt.

RETURN

Son of a bitch.

ELEVEN

Henry and I walked out of the police station after giving our statements. We descended the front stairs and saw Laura at the bottom of the steps. Her red pickup truck was parked behind her in the street. We stopped in front of her. She had a look of concern on her face.

"Dad. Charlie. What happened?", inquired Laura.

"Sweetie, we're fine.", assured Henry.

"Deputy Harris told me that Tyler pulled a knife on you guys in the middle of Lenny's!", exclaimed Laura.

I nodded.

"You should've seen Charlie.", added Henry. "He handled himself pretty well."

RETURN

I was flattered by Henry's comment but still abashed about the whole incident. Laura hugged me tight and I hugged her back.

"I'm glad you're okay.", she said and then she let go of me.

"Me, too. My head is hurting. Could we go back to the farm, please?"

"Sure, let's call it a night.", she agreed.

I walked up to her truck and got in the passenger side. I closed the door and held my head.

"I'll see you both back at the house.", said Henry. He walked away from us and disappeared around the corner of the police station into the adjacent parking lot. Laura got in the truck and started it up. She drove around the square and then turned on to her road. She continued down the way and we were back at the farm within a couple minutes. She pulled into the driveway then parked the truck and killed the engine. I got out and started to head towards my room. She got out of the truck after I did.

"Laura, I'm going to hit the hay. I'm beat.", I groaned.

"You don't want dinner?", she asked.

"Nah, I don't have much of an appetite right now. I think I'll just get some sleep instead."

"Charlie, wait."

I turned and looked at her. She walked up to me and grabbed my hand. She looked into my eyes.

"Charlie... I want you to know that I'm so sorry about this whole thing with Tyler. I didn't think it would get to a point like this that it would affect other people close to me.", she pleaded.

"Laura, it's not your fault.", I told her.

"I know but I can't help but feel responsible for it just because Tyler is obsessed with me and he can't get over the fact that I will never be with him again. I want you to know that I care about you deeply, Charlie. I don't want to lose you.", Laura confided in me.

"I care about you too, Laura. Don't you worry about Tyler. He won't be bothering you forever and I won't let him hurt you.", I assured her.

She stepped a little closer to me and gave me a soft kiss on the lips. We saw the lights of Henry's truck approaching the driveway and she pulled away from me. I smiled at her and she smiled back.

"Good night, Laura.", I said.

"Good night, Charlie.", she said.

I walked back to the guest room and entered through the front door. I closed it behind me and didn't bother with turning on the lights to see. My familiarity with the room had become comfortable enough that I felt confident to navigate through it without bumping into any objects. I went into the bedroom and kicked off my boots. After I let my feet breathe, I crashed on the bed and just laid there with my thoughts and a mild throbbing of my head. The moonlight was creeping through the window as I was just staring at the ceiling. I shut my eyes but my thoughts were racing. A lot has happened since the past weekend.

RETURN

The memory of my parents at my childhood home appeared before me. My mother was cooking soup in the kitchen and I saw my father approach her and hug her from behind. I looked at the both of them smiling then they turned their heads towards me.

I heard voices outside and I opened my eyes. I looked at the dresser and saw a plate covered with a chrome top. I sat up and put my feet on the floor. I walked over to the dresser and there was a note next to the plate that read:

Just in case you get your appetite
back in the middle of the night.
XOXO,
Laura

I lifted the top and saw a skinless chicken breast with some broccoli and a mound of mashed potatoes with a pool of gravy in the center. I took a couple bites of the meal then covered the plate again. It was delicious but I still wasn't very hungry.

Without warning, I recognized Henry and Laura's voices outside. I heard them talking about something where it seemed to be getting emotional. I walked up to the window and peeked out from behind the curtain. It was now easier to understand what they were saying.

"What about Tyler, Dad? He could've seriously hurt you tonight. I'm afraid of what he could do to you or Charlie."

"Sweetie, I've been through far worse than what Tyler

could do. Don't worry about me. I'm not going anywhere."

"That still doesn't make me feel better."

"I don't expect it to. However, you can't let fear of the unknown keep you from living your life.", said Henry.

"I know. You're right. I just... I don't know what I would do if I lost you or Charlie." I saw her start to cry.

Henry hugged Laura. "Sweetie, it's okay.", affirmed Henry. She continued to cry into his chest.

Henry was trying to calm her down and was holding her head gently.

"Laura, you've become a strong and caring woman. Your mother would be very proud of you.", Henry said. Laura took her face out of Henry's chest and she wiped away tears.

"I miss Mom.", she sobbed.

"I miss her, too.", divulged Henry.

He patted her on the back as she kept sobbing.

"I know she would've liked Charlie.", Henry added.

Laura let out a brief chuckle and pulled away from Henry.

"Yeah, she would've.", she stated.

"I like him, too.", Henry admitted. "If you had children with him, I would be the proudest grandfather."

"Dad..."

"Laura, I may be getting older but I'm not getting stupid. I was young once, too. I know what it's like to have those feelings and to act upon those feelings. I know how it is to be intimate with someone you care about. Plus, I saw you kiss him as I was coming up the driveway.", Henry told her.

Laura laughed and she wiped away more tears.

"Nothing gets past you.", she jokingly said. Henry smiled.

"If there is some connection between you two, which is rarer than you think, the best thing to do is not to ignore it. Some people in their lifetime never get that opportunity.", disclosed Henry.

"Thank you, Dad. I love you.", Laura said as she smiled wide and hugged him again.

"I love you too, Sweetie." He hugged her tight then they let go of each other. Henry put his arm around Laura and she put her arm around Henry then both of them headed back towards the house.

I pulled away from the window and let the curtain fall back into place. I laid back on the bed and thought about everything that Henry had said to her. The fact that Laura cared about me as much as I cared about her began to relax me. The chemistry between us was definitely there and it felt right.

She is smart, beautiful, funny, confident, compassionate... and there are so many other things about her that I love. What wasn't to love about her? Everyone in town liked her. She's made me feel so welcome. She's been looking out for me ever since I got here. It is an added bonus that I also find her to be a very sexy woman.

I began to feel at ease and I closed my eyes again. I was slowly starting to drift away into sleep.

I thought of Lenny's again. I was just sitting at the bar and it was completely empty. It was a moment of contemplation and I was just staring into my glass of beer. I only heard the sound of the ceiling fan spinning away. There were footsteps echoing behind the bar that were coming closer to me. I noticed a shadow that was looming over me. I looked up and it was Heidi? She was dressed as the bartender.

    I was shocked from the appearance that I moved back slightly.

    "You need to wake up!", she yelled.

    She picked up the glass in front of me and threw the beer in my face.

RETURN

TWELVE

I woke up. There was the sound of a horse galloping nearby. I looked towards the window and saw that the sun was up. I looked at the clock and it was quarter after 8. The newspaper was sitting there on the night stand and I unfolded it to display the front page. Today was Friday November 8th. The festival was tomorrow. I took the blanket off of me and put my feet on the floor. I felt the chill against the bottom of my feet even though I was wearing socks. It was colder in here than it had been the previous days. It finally felt like November. I put on my jeans, a t-shirt, the boots and my jacket. I went outside to get some fresh air. It was a bit nippy but I could feel the sun on my face.

I heard the horse galloping behind me and went to the other side of the barn. I saw Laura riding the horse all over the farm. She was wearing her navy blue cap and I saw her auburn hair sticking out of the back of it. She was wearing a jacket along with her boots and jeans under leather chaps. She really was a cowgirl and she took my breath away.

I walked up to the fence surrounding the pen and leaned against it as I continued to watch her. She rode that horse to the end of one field then circled around and began to ride fast along the crops. When she got near the end of the field, she slowed down and turned towards me.

She waved to me and commanded the horse to go towards the barn. Laura and the horse slowly galloped towards the barn and entered the barn through an opening next to the pen on the other side from me. They both entered the pen from the barn and then Laura stopped the horse. That horse was huge and she had a surefire look on her face that she was in control.

"Morning, Sleepyhead.", she playfully said.
"Morning. You're up early."
"Well, it was a perfect time for a ride.", she answered. She dismounted the horse and held on to him.
"You wanna try?", she asked me.
"I've never rode a horse before.", I said.
"Nothing to it. Come into the pen.", she directed.
I jogged around the perimeter of the pen and proceeded through the same opening where Laura and the

horse entered. As I entered the barn, I turned left and walked through the opening to the pen. Laura signaled me to come to her as she was holding on the horse.

"Alright, just grab the horn on the saddle and put your left foot right here in the stirrup."

I followed her instructions.

"Now push yourself up from the stirrup, lift your other leg over him and into the other stirrup.", she advised. I did that and I was sitting on top of the horse. I felt like I was ten feet tall.

"Feeling good?", she asked me.

"Yeah, I'm good.", I confirmed.

"Alright, a few things to know here. 'Whoa' means stop. 'Walk' means walk. 'Easy' means slow down. 'Let's go' means run. Hold on to the reins. Got it?", she said.

I nodded. Laura looked at the horse and said "Go easy." The horse started walking slowly around the pen. "This is great! I'm actually riding a horse!", I said with a jovial fervor. Laura had a wide smile on her face. I could tell she was passionate about this. We were circling back around to Laura. "Howdy, Cowgirl.", I jested while making a hat tipping gesture. "Hello, Cowboy." she joked back. The horse did another lap around the pen. "How do I look?", I asked Laura. "Like you were born to ride.", she happily said.

The horse was nearing Laura again and I gave the command with a slight tug on the reins.

"Whoa."

The horse stopped. Laura grabbed a hold of the reins. I took my right leg out of the stirrup and moved it back to the left side of the horse. I got my right foot on the ground successfully and got my left foot out of the stirrup without falling.

"Nice first ride.", she complimented.

"I make it look easy, right?", I teased. Laura laughed. Laura then scratched the horse behind the ears and told him he was a good boy. She took the saddle off of the horse and started walking him back to the barn. I began to walk with her.

"Here, let me help you out.", I said as I reached for the saddle and she gave it to me.

"Thank you.", Laura said.

"Of course.", I told her.

"Just set it on the table inside.", Laura commanded.

We entered the barn and I placed the saddle on the table as Laura had instructed. She escorted the horse towards a stable near the opening to the pen. In front of the stable, the horse stopped. I watched her carefully with how she took the bridle off of the horse and then Laura directed him into the stable.

"So why was this morning a perfect time to ride?", I asked as I was genuinely curious. She developed an apprehensive look on her face and I had a feeling it had nothing to do with horses. I could tell she was trying to process what she was going to say next while intentionally not trying to look at me. As soon as the horse was inside, Laura closed the gate on the stable.

She walked over to the table and set the bridle down next to the saddle. A melancholy expression began to form on her face as she looked at me. She inhaled slowly and started her story.

"My mother died on the very last day of August. It was unusually cold that same night and I saw the first frost before Autumn the very next morning. When I saw that frost on the ground, it hit me that my mother is gone and she's not coming back. So I saw that frost again on the ground this morning and it made me think of her. I go for a ride because it clears my head and centers me.", she explained.

"That's beautiful. I wish I had an outlet like that to help me whenever I miss my parents, which is every day.", I said.

She walked over to me and hugged me. I hugged her back. As much as I loved holding her, I felt like I should change the subject. I looked back at where the horse was and saw the name plate above the stable. It said "Goliath."

"Goliath, huh? So it's not just a clever name.", I joked. Laura chuckled.

"Yeah, he's my baby boy.", she said. The horse was a behemoth.

She looked at Goliath and he huffed and puffed. Laura looked back at me and we were still holding each other. She softly said, "Thank you for listening to me. I've never been this personal with anyone before. Not even with Tyler. I feel this strong connection to you."

"I feel connected to you, too, like we're... kindred spirits. I deeply care about you and I'm crazy about you.", I confessed.

I temporarily panicked from being so blunt and

forthcoming. I didn't want to freak her out but I decided it's a little too late to take back what I just said so I might as well go with it.

I continued on, "I just want to be open and honest with you and you to be that way with me. I want you to be comfortable saying whatever you need to say and I want to be there to listen. I'm hoping you would do the same for me as well."

"I would.", she said. She went in and kissed me. I passionately kissed her back and we locked lips for a few seconds. We both pulled away and looked at each other. "And I'm crazy about you, too.", she added.

YES!

I smiled back at her and I kissed her again. She was deeply kissing me back. I felt her grab my butt and the horse loudly squealed. She broke away from our kiss and started laughing. She turned and looked at Goliath.

"Hey! I still love you, too.", she cheerily said to the horse. She looked back at me and broke away from the hug.

"Okay, I need to go shower. I probably stink.", she said.

"You're sexy either way.", I said aloud.

Oh, shit. I just said that out loud. What the hell is up with me?

"Um... that was rude of me. I apologize.", I quickly added.

She smiled wide and then gave me a quick kiss on the lips. She went over to my ear and whispered. "You're sexy, too. FYI, dirty talk makes me very horny." She backed away

RETURN

from me, turned around and walked out of the barn. I watched her perfect ass in those Levi's move away from me and disappear out into the sunlight.

I earned the right to look at that ass now.

Goliath huffed and puffed then shook his head. I looked at him and sarcastically said "What?". The horse made more noises as I walked away from the stable and out of the barn.

After exiting the barn, I saw Henry in the garage. He was sitting on a stool in front of a workbench and he wasn't dressed in cowboy attire. He was wearing jeans with various paint stains that looked worn out. He was also wearing a jacket and a black baseball cap. I saw he was crafting something small made out of wood. It grabbed my attention so I made my way over to him. I noticed he was also wearing glasses.

"Morning, Henry."

"Morning, Charlie."

"What are you making?", I asked him.

"This is a small replica of the box in town.", said Henry.

"That old iron one with the dials and the crazy riddle?", I guessed.

"That same one.", Henry admitted.

"No one has ever solved the riddle?"

"Hammond probably. But he's dead, so good luck with that.", Henry remarked. I laughed. I sat down on a chair near him and he was just gently smoothing out the miniature box with some sandpaper. "What do you know about the box?", I politely asked.

Henry stopped sanding. He looked at me then started, "Well, whatever it is, it's very heavy. That box does not move, *at all*. Also, there is a circular area with a six inch diameter on the very center top of the box that looks to be a separate metallic component from the actual box. My guess is that is where the box opens. All of the dials are only zero through nine." He went back to sanding the replica.

"Peculiar.", I said.

"No shit, right?", he agreed then added "For a nearly two hundred year old iron box, it surprisingly doesn't have a lot of rust."

"What are your thoughts on the riddle?", I asked.

"You got me there, kid. I'm stumped by that. What do you know about Jeffrey Fitzgerald Hammond?" He stopped sanding and placed the sandpaper down. He took off his glasses and started wiping the sawdust from them that had accumulated.

"Well... he founded the town, he loved books, there's the secret place under the lighthouse, the painting, the table, the box, the town library..." I ran out of things to say.

Henry said, "Well if you want to figure out the riddle, I'd guess that's where you start." *He has a point.*

"So what's the box for?", I asked.

"Gift for someone.", he said. He put his glasses back on and picked up the sandpaper.

"Laura?", I cheerfully asked.

"Keep your mouth shut, Charlie.", Henry sternly said.

He went back to sanding the replica.

"I won't tell her. I promise.", I promised. I felt the weather start to warm up. I looked at the Buffalo Bills clock hanging on the wall in the garage and it was almost 1:30. Time moves so easily around here.

"Henry, thanks for the conversation. This has been very educational."

"See ya later.", he said.

I walked up to the house and Laura walked out with her navy blue cap on, green t-shirt tucked into jeans and boots. *Looking like her sexy self. She's incredible.*

"Hey", we both said to each other. We stopped and stood there in front of the door.

"Michelle and Derek are having a barbeque later at their house and they invited us."

I wanted to go back to the library but I guess that can wait. I like spending time with her anyway.

"Sounds great. Do I have time to hop in the shower?", I questioned.

"Plenty.", she reckoned.

"Good. I probably stink.", I pointed out.

She gently grabbed my face and gave me a small sweet kiss on the lips. She got close to my ear and whispered, "You're still sexy."

I felt myself get excited down there.

She walked away from me with a smile on her face and went out towards the barn. I went in the house and into the bathroom as quickly as possible to avoid anyone who could see the pants tent I just pitched.

THIRTEEN

I walked out of the bathroom fully dressed and finally with a clean shave. I stopped into the laundry room. I dropped the towel into the hamper, walked through the kitchen and went outside. Laura was walking out of the barn and she was headed in my direction. I decided to meet her half way.

"So when are we going to the barbeque?", I asked.

"We can go whenever. They've probably already started partying. Lots of people in the town are going to be partying this weekend.", she said.

"I'm ready when you are.", I announced.

"Well, let's head out then.", she proposed. Laura

looked over at the garage. Henry was still working on the replica.

"Dad, we're going to Michelle and Derek's for their party."

"You two have fun.", Henry responded. Laura looked back at me and said "Follow me. We'll take a shortcut." She started to walk across the farm and towards the woods. I followed her lead. As we were getting closer to the woods, I noticed that there was a path and I had concluded that's where we were going. We entered the narrow path and we were greeted by the elements of the forest. We continued on the trek passing by all sorts of flora and fauna as well as watching my step while staying on this narrow path. I saw an opening at the end of the path and there was a clearing ahead. As soon as we got out to the clearing, I noticed that I've seen this before.

The painting in the underground room of the lighthouse.
"So here it is.", Laura addressed.

"Strange. Is this man-made or has it always been like this?", I inquired.

"I honestly have no idea.", Laura confessed.

I saw the boulders lined up from left to right in a straight line. Laura continued to walk and I followed her. When we got around the straight line, I noticed the boulders in the shape of the ellipse. We continued around the ellipse and walked into another path that went through the woods. Laura grabbed my hand and led me on the path. We stayed on this narrow path for a good amount of yards, and walked around a small mud pit that was right in the center of the path.

Shortly after that, we passed by a tree trunk that look like it was split in half with a stick of dynamite and moved on to a path that was surrounded by tall grass. We got to the end of the path and we were in the back yard of a very large wooden house. It looked like one of those flashy upscale lodges that you could rent for a week.

There was music blasting off of the deck facing us. "Hey!", a voice yelled off the deck. I saw Michelle climb down the stairs from the deck and run over to us with a beer in her hand. Laura greeted her with, "Hey Girlie!" She went to hug Laura and then she hugged me.

"So glad you guys could make it!", Michelle said with a lot of enthusiasm. "I hope you brought your appetites! Derek is working his magic on the grill.", Michelle added. "I'm starving.", I said to appease her.

"Awesome. Well come on, everyone's on the deck.", she cheerfully said. We followed her up to the deck. I recognized Derek on the grill and there were a few other people I did not know. They seemed to know Laura as when she walked up there, everyone was yelling "Hey!" and went to greet her. She made the rounds introducing me and I shook everyone's hand, with success I might add, and everyone seemed really friendly. It made me feel like the man of the hour for two minutes.

I walked over to Derek who was hard at work grilling hot dogs and just threw on a few beef patties.

"Hey, Derek.", I said.

"Hey, man! What's going on? There's beer in every cooler out here. Help yourself. Could you grab me one while you're at it?", he said.

I reached into the cooler next to me and pulled out three beers. I gave one to Derek and he thanked me. I walked backed over to Laura and gave her the other. She took it from me and popped the can open.

"Thanks, Babe.", she said.

"You're welcome, Babe.", I echoed. I popped my can open. We lightly knocked our cans together. We both said, "Cheers" and then we took a gulp of our beers.

"So, Charlie...", Derek started, "... what do you do for a living?". I smiled with my beer in my mouth and I saw Laura form a smile on her face as she was trying not to spit out hers. I swallowed the gulp of lager.

"I guess you could say I'm in between jobs right now.", I answered.

"Oh yeah? What did you do before?", Derek asked.

"I worked at Red Wheel Products.", I told him.

"Ah. I just happen to know someone that used to work there. He told me the boss is a real dick.", Derek said.

Laura and I both laughed.

"He's correct.", I verified. Derek took a sip of his beer.

"So what are you going to do now?", Derek asked.

"I guess I haven't thought about it. I've been preoccupied.", I conceded. I looked at Laura out of the corner of my eye with a smile then she pursed her lips and blew a kiss at me.

Then I had an idea.

"Maybe I should just move here.", I said. Laura looked at me with a glow in her eyes like she really wanted that. Derek looked me and said "Well, if you decide to do that let me know. I can help you with finding work, maybe even a place."

"Thank you. I appreciate that.", I said with the utmost gratitude.

"You're welcome. Now go enjoy yourself. I need to be a Jedi master on this grill right now.", he said.

I walked over to everyone else and began to mingle and socialize with Laura. I met Ryan, who was sporting a camouflage T-shirt along with a Buffalo Sabres hat. We discussed hockey as I was also a fan. I got a little bit annoyed of the fact that he kept saying that the Sabres needed to trade to get Sidney Crosby. Ryan seemed like an alright guy but his knowledge of hockey was a bit lacking.

I also met his girlfriend Michaela and she was rocking a shirt that said *Kiss My Country Ass*. Laura and her were chatting up about various things from horseback riding to music. Michelle started pouring shots of whiskey. She was handing them out to everyone. "C'mon! Shots!", she announced to the group. She handed the last two shots to Derek and me. My shot glass had the phrase *Touch Me Where I Pee.* on the side.

Cute.

Michelle raised her shot glass and then she spoke. "I want to thank all of you for coming out and celebrating with us. To good friends and good fun."

"Here, here." said Derek. We raised our glasses and downed our shots. I felt a mild burn and chased it with my beer. I usually did not take shots but what the hell. It's not like I can go anywhere anyway. I looked over at Derek and he was taking the last of the food off of the grill. "Soup's on!", he shouted. He set the tray of food on a dining table near us.

We made our way over and grabbed some paper plates and helped ourselves. There were hot dogs, hamburgers, ribs, chicken and potato salad. We began to feast and the food was outstanding.

Is everyone an amazing cook in this town? I love the food here.

We were washing our food down with beers and the occasional shot. I was more than halfway through my meal when I had the notion to say something.

"Thanks, Derek. This is fantastic. The ribs are so tender.", I said as I went to work on my plate of barbeque.

"No problem and thank you. Yeah, it's an old family recipe. My father owns the barbeque restaurant in town."

"Oh, yeah? What's it called?", I asked.

"BBQ HQ.", he said. I chortled at the name.

"That's a great name! Catchy."

"Thank you. My grandfather opened the place a long time ago and it's been the family business since then.", Derek disclosed.

"Well, looks like I have another reason to stick around in town longer. I'll have to stop by and have some more.", I said. Laura set her plate down. She got up from her seat and walked down the stairs of the deck while looking at her phone. My meal had been cleared from my plate so I wiped my fingers with my napkin then stood up and tossed the paper plate in the trash. I walked down the stairs after her. I turned a corner and saw her talking on the phone. I started walking toward her then she hung up the phone.

"Everything okay?", I asked. "You sort of just took off."

"Yeah, everything is fine. I was just talking with my dad."

"Good. Glad to hear it.", I said. She leaned towards me and kissed me on the cheek.

"It's really sweet of you that you were concerned about me. It's refreshing, too.", Laura told me. She grabbed my hand and we walked back to the deck. Another song came on and it was more slow paced then the last song.

"Oh! I love this song!", exclaimed Laura. The tune sounded familiar. It was a slow rock and blues hybrid song with a small folky vibe to it. It was being sung by some guy with a slight melodic rasp in his voice. I couldn't figure out who this was that was singing but I knew I had heard it before.

It sounds like this one Canadian rock band I've heard but their name escapes me. I've heard this song multiple times before. Why can't I think of the name?

We were still holding hands so I pulled her close to me and put my other arm around her waist. She looked pleasantly surprised. I led and we slow danced right there on the lawn. We looked into each other's eyes while keeping the rhythm.

"You're a good dancer.", she said.

"Well, I've done this once or twice before.", I teased.

She smiled at me appearing to appreciate the joke.

"Well, you just scored some big brownie points with me. I like it when a man can be strong and sensitive at the same time.", Laura said.

I realized that it seemed to be getting darker. I took a brief look at the horizon and the sun appeared to be setting.

Time here goes by so quickly it seems.

I kept dancing with her and I got lost in her eyes. Laura noticed and she smiled at me.

"What?", she said as she started to blush.

"You're so beautiful. It's just so incredible to meet you after what I've been through over the past week."

"Oh yeah? So, how did you and Heidi break up?", Laura asked me.

"I don't know if I should talk about that.", I pleaded.

"Hey, you can trust me. Also, I was open and honest with you this morning in the barn. You said you wanted to be open and honest with me. So live up to your words and be open and honest with me.", Laura said.

She's right. I said that. Suck it up and tell her.

I took a deep breath and hoped this would go over well.

"Recently, an ex-boyfriend of hers was making his presence known in our lives. I had a bad feeling about him but she was on good terms with him and she's known him longer than she's known me so I didn't want to come across as the bad guy. Shortly, after he came around she received photos of me with another woman."

A look of shock formed on Laura's face.

"Laura, I swear on the graves of my parents that I was not in those photos and I did not cheat on her. Those photos were altered. Computers do lots of crazy shit nowadays but I digress. Anyway, Heidi did not believe me and we fought over it. When I mentioned my suspicions of him, it only made the situation worse. It was a horrible fight. She said she did not want to have a life together with anyone who would treat her friends this way. She dumped me and told me that she never wanted to see me again. When she said that, it tore something out of me. I stormed out of our apartment and then I got to here.", I explained. After I finished my story, I hung my head in embarrassment.

Laura grabbed my chin and turned my face upwards to hers. She kissed me.

"I believe you." she said.

"Thank you. That means a lot to me.", I confessed.

I felt so relieved and the connection between us seemed to get instantly stronger. I didn't want this moment to end and I decided not to interrupt it with any more words.

I leaned in and kissed her. We held our lips together and then the song ended. A more upbeat song came on afterwards. We ended our kiss. Derek walked by us with a bunch of folding chairs. "I'm starting a bonfire if you're interested.", he said. Suddenly, I saw another group of people coming from the front of the house and towards the deck. Michelle came down from the deck and greeted everyone. She introduced us to all the new people that were joining us. I had a good buzz going so I couldn't remember some of their names to tell you the truth.

    The music kept blasting and there were girls dancing on the deck. We told jokes. The people on the deck were playing games of beer pong and I saw Ryan and Michaela playing horseshoes with another couple. Before I knew it, the sun was down and the moon was shining bright. The house lights came on when the darkness seemed to be profound.

    Derek set up the folding chairs a good distance away from the bonfire pit. The pit was loaded with broken pallets and miscellaneous tinder. He threw some gas on the pile and lit the fire at one corner. I saw the little fire burning. It eventually traveled towards the center and then the whole pile went aflame.

    He went back to the house. Laura and I made our way to the bonfire and sat in a couple chairs. We turned our heads and saw Derek coming back with a guitar case. He sat down in a chair and pulled the guitar out of the case. He began to tune it. Once it sounded good to him, he started jamming out around the fire. Michelle came up to us and sat down next to Derek. More people began to join us.

    Derek starting playing some Led Zeppelin on the guitar. I recognized he was playing 'Tangerine.'

    "Good choice.", I said. Derek nodded with approval.

Everyone began singing the song around the fire. I loved that they had great taste in music.

Derek pulled out some other classics from that era as well. Everyone seemed to know the words. I was enjoying myself thoroughly then Laura reached for my head and kissed me again.

I felt pretty drunk and I could tell Laura had a good buzz going. Laura looked at the clock on her phone, as well as I, and we noticed that it was nearly midnight.

"Ah, it's getting late.", Laura implied. "Maybe we should get going. I have to get up fairly early tomorrow for the festival."

"Okie dokie.", I responded. We walked over to Michelle and Derek who were sitting in front of the fire. "Hey, we got to get going, guys. Thanks for having us.", Laura said.

"Yes, thank you so much. It was great.", I added.

"You guys are very welcome!", Michelle happily said. Michelle got up from her chair and hugged Laura and then she hugged me.

"You guys take it easy.", I replied.

"You too. Get home safe.", responded Derek. We both waved at them and walked away from the fire and back towards the path in the woods. Laura grabbed my hand and we walked onto the path. The path was well lit by the moonlight. We went around the small mud pit and walked along the path until we got near the opening. Laura stopped under a tree then turned around to kiss me. I tripped over a branch on the ground and fell into her. She lost her balance and also fell down with me into the clearing. My head fell into her breasts. We both started laughing. I lifted my head up and stared into her eyes. I lustfully kissed her and stuck my tongue in her mouth. She was slowly massaging it with her own tongue. I felt her reach around my waist and felt her hands gently move down my body.

I heard a growl from behind me. We stopped kissing. I turned around and I saw a wolf probably about 20 yards behind us that was slowly approaching us. He was keeping his eyes on us and letting his growl be heard. The wolf's presence gave me a brief relapse into sobriety. I stood up cautiously while keeping my eyes on the wolf. I held out my hand and Laura grabbed on to it as I helped her up from the ground.

"There are wolves around here?", I asked Laura.

"It's pretty rare but they've been seen around here before.", Laura confirmed. "Okay", she started, "keep facing him and move back slowly away from the wolf." We started doing that while holding each other's hands. The wolf kept a steady pace while following us.

We began to gradually step backwards around the boulders then started to run around them in order to get to the other path. I saw the wolf take off after us. We ran around the curve and when we got to the other path we saw another wolf there waiting for us and growling.

"Oh, shit.", we both said.

I noticed a small log on the ground near my foot. I picked it up and gave it to Laura. "Here, hit the bastard if he gets near you.", I said. Laura grabbed the log and held it up in a defensive stance. We put our backs to each other. "Get out of here! Help!", Laura yelled.

I saw the first wolf moving towards me. I looked behind my back and saw the other one coming towards Laura. I tried to come up with a way to scare them off.

What scares off wolves? Appearing more dangerous?

I stood up on my toes, lifted up my arms, and loudly growled at them while showing my teeth. I was hoping that would intimidate them but they just came closer. I did it one more time to the wolf that was facing me. I immediately turned around to the other wolf and did the same thing to him.

A gunshot went off and I saw a burst of blood spray out of the side of the wolf's head. The wolf collapsed to the ground. I turned around and saw the other wolf take off. We heard leaves rustle and footsteps coming closer. Henry appeared with a rifle in his hands. We both breathed a sigh of relief.

"Are you two alright?", Henry asked. He ejected a shell out of the rifle and then knelt down to pick it up off the ground.

"Thank you, Dad. I'm okay.", said Laura.

"I'm alright too. You saved our asses. Thanks.", I said.

"No problem. Let's get back to the house. We'll call Jack and he can call Animal Control to get rid of the carcass.", said Henry.

RETURN

We followed him back to the farm. Laura and I held hands the whole way. I was grateful that Henry showed up when he did. We were still together and I knew that this could've ended in a much worse way.

We walked up to the porch and I sat down in one of the rocking chairs. I felt a throbbing in my head and I needed a minute off of my feet.

My head hurts again.

Now I remember that band from when I was dancing with Laura. Big Wreck. Exactly like totaling my car. I've heard them before. I like that band. I know that band. How did I forget that?

FOURTEEN

Jack pulled into the driveway and parked his car. A truck pulled into the driveway and parked behind him. I was very surprised by how fast they got here. It seemed like only two minutes. Jack stepped out of his car and walked up to all of us who were sitting on the front porch.

"Henry.", Jack casually said. Henry stood up from his rocking chair.

"Jack. Sorry to call you this late.", Henry said.

"No problem. Where's the wolf?", Jack asked. Henry pointed in the direction of the path.

"Just on the path down there near the boulders.", explained Henry. The other gentleman took notice and he walked in that direction with a large flashlight and some sort of large bag in his arms.

"Thanks for the call, Henry. We'll get the carcass out of here shortly."

"Thanks, Jack."

"There's also another reason why I came out here.", Jack divulged. He paused. "Tyler made bail." I saw Henry's face become cold.

"Seriously, Jack? He's reckless and dangerous. I've had enough of him harassing my daughter.", Henry said with a bit of anger.

"Henry, I know and I'm sorry. I really am.", Jack apologetically said.

"What if he comes after me?", I asked.

"Well, let me know. He has violated his probation so he's looking at some jail time. I don't think he's going to try and start any more trouble.", Jack said. I wanted to believe him but I had a feeling in my gut that statement probably did not reflect the truth.

"Plus, from what I saw last time, it seemed like you handled yourself pretty well, Charlie.", Jack added. I found humor in what he said but it wasn't enough to calm my nerves. Tyler clearly had some issues. Laura grabbed my hand and looked at me. She smiled at me. That made me feel better.

"Every police officer will be on duty tomorrow for the festival so don't worry.", Jack assured us.

"That's only four people, Jack.", Henry said.

"Four is enough for one person. Tyler's not that

smart.", Jack rebutted. Jack got that right but less intelligence leads to more recklessness. Henry loudly exhaled.

"Fine. I swear if I have to take him out myself to protect my daughter, I'm putting that on you.", Henry cautioned. He turned around and walked into the house. He slammed the door behind him. Laura stood up and looked at Jack.

"Thank you for letting us know, Sheriff.", Laura politely said.

"Don't thank me. It was the right thing to let you know. I'm not happy about Tyler being out either but the law is the law. I know Tyler is an asshole but him being an asshole is not illegal."

"True, but it also seems he doesn't have much regard for the law.", I shot back.

"You're right, Charlie. I know his history but he has to do something illegal for me to do anything about it. This whole Tyler thing will be over and done with soon and I know that Henry will eventually cool off. He just needs some time." I saw the gentleman with the bag coming from the path in the woods. It looked like he collected the wolf. He was approaching his truck. "We're all set, Sheriff.", the gentleman said.

"Thanks, Hodges.", spoke Jack. Hodges swung the bag and placed it into the back of the truck. He took off a pair of gloves he was wearing and also threw those in the back of the truck. Jack asked, "Will I see you two tomorrow at the festival?"

"We'll both be there.", Laura confirmed.

"You flying the blimp for the air show again?", asked Jack.

"Yes, indeed.", Laura said with an air of confidence.

"Always an entertaining spectacle. You two have a good night.", Jack said. He walked back to his car, opened the door and got in. Hodges entered his truck.

"You too, Sheriff.", I replied. I waved.

"Thank you, Sheriff.", Laura responded.

Hodges started up his truck and backed out of the driveway. Jack followed suit and then they were gone. Laura turned and looked at me.

"Hell of a way to end the day, right?", she commented.

"Yeah, for real.", I agreed. She walked up to me and hugged me tight. She loosened her grip, looked up at me and said, "Don't worry about, Tyler. I won't let him hurt you." I chuckled and I looked into her eyes.

"I won't let him hurt you, too. I promise."

I meant it. She kissed me. She grabbed my hand and we walked back to the barn. She started, "So, what did you do to Tyler in the bar?"

Oh boy. I sighed.

"I smashed him in the face with a telephone. I knocked out two of his teeth.", I told her.

Laura's jaw dropped.

"It was what I had to do to protect myself. He was swinging a pool cue at me and it was all I had.", I explained. She started chuckling. "I hope you said something cool.", she expressed.

"I said 'It's for you.'" She burst out laughing even harder. We got to the door on the side of the barn. We stopped and held hands then we stared into each other's eyes.

"I love how you make me laugh. It makes you more sexy.", she confessed.

"Same here.", I told her. She kissed me again and we had a passionate kiss to close out the night. We broke contact from our lips. She said, "Get some rest. We have a busy day tomorrow."

"Yeah, that sounds like a good idea.", I replied.

"I'll come by and see you before I head to the festival tomorrow. We'll go over the game plan and do breakfast.", she said.

"Looking forward to it.", I said

"Good night, Handsome.", she said.

"Good night, Gorgeous.", I said and then I kissed her.

She kissed me hard and grabbed my butt. I figured I would return the favor and so I grabbed her butt. Wow, it was firm and I loved it. She backed away from me and started walking back to the house.

"Save your energy, cowboy. You're gonna need it.", she said. I watched her go back to the house.

Oh. My. God. She drives me wild.

I went back into the guest room and closed the door. I entered the bedroom and kicked off my boots. I stripped off my clothes again and crashed on the bed. I put the blanket over me and tried to get some sleep. Tomorrow couldn't get here soon enough. I closed my eyes. All I could think of was

RETURN

Laura. The thought of her put me at peace.

My peace was abruptly interrupted by another thought. I was standing on the edge of the cliff staring at the lake. I saw the lighthouse to my left and some woods along the edge of the cliff to my right. It was eerily calm out here. I was standing underneath gray cloudy skies. The water was strangely still. I heard a growl behind me. I turned around and it was the other wolf.
    He showed his teeth at me.
    He was angry and he was drooling.
    He wanted revenge for his companion. Then it began to speak in Uncle Greg's voice.
    "Snap out of it!", the wolf yelled.
    The wolf lunged at me and I went over the cliff. I was plunging head first towards the water and I pierced the liquid darkness.

FIFTEEN

I woke up. I took a deep breath then jettisoned the air out of my lungs.
What is with these dreams I'm having?
I heard the door open. Laura walked in all dressed up in her jeans and boots looking ready to cowgirl it up. She was wearing a tucked in button-down turquoise shirt and sporting that massive buckle that would be big enough to kill... hah... a wolf.
I looked at the clock. It was quarter after 9. "C'mon sleepyhead. Breakfast is ready.", she said. She leaned down and kissed me. She held my head and lovingly stared at me.
"Good way to start out the morning.", I jested. She

smiled wide. She stood back up and exited the room. I sat up, got out of bed and walked into the bathroom. I looked in the mirror and analyzed the cut on my head. It was looking better. I did my business, washed my hands and got dressed.

I walked up to the house and entered through the front door. I walked into the dining room and Laura was sitting at the table drinking coffee and reading the paper. Henry was also sitting there at the table. He was also dressed in his Western attire and he was enjoying his eggs and ham. He turned and saw me.

"Morning, Charlie."

"Morning, Henry."

I sat down in the empty spot next to Laura with the plate that was covered with a chrome top. I lifted the cover off of the plate. Laura had given me some scrambled eggs, hash browns, a ham steak and a couple pieces of wheat toast. There was a small bowl of strawberries in front of me along with a glass of orange juice to accompany my meal.

Laura picked up a metallic pot. "Coffee?", she asked.

"Please.", I responded. She poured the coffee into a white mug that said *MURICA* in red and blue letters. I chuckled.

"I like the mug.", I expressed. Laura smiled.

"That old thing? Yeah, it's amusing.", she revealed. She put the pot back down on the table and went back to reading the paper. I started on my breakfast. I took the first bite and let out a groan of pleasure. The ham steak was juicy and succulent. The eggs were delicious and the hash browns were cooked just to the right amount of crispiness.

"So what's the plan for today?", I asked.

"Really soon, I need to go into town so I can get ready for the air show at noon. After that's done, then we can just hang out at the festival all day.", Laura explained as she was reading the paper.

"Simple and sweet. Sounds good to me.", I approved.

"You can ride into town with me.", offered Henry.

"Thank you, Henry.", I said. Henry nodded. I took a sip of my coffee. Laura set the newspaper down on the table. "I got to go.", she acknowledged. She stood up from the table.

"Breakfast is great. Thank you.", I told her. She kissed me on the cheek and responded with, "You're welcome. I'll see you later."

"Definitely. Looking forward to it.", I told her.

She walked over to Henry and gave him a kiss on the cheek.

"See you later, Dad.", Laura said.

"See you later, Sweetie.", spoke Henry. Laura exited the room and I heard her leave the house. I picked up the newspaper and saw the date on it. Saturday November 9th. The front page had a story about the festival and another story regarding an upcoming election for a Senator.

I didn't sleep through Election Day? I thought it was the first Tuesday after the first Monday in November?

I set the paper back down on the table then looked at the clock on the wall. It was a little after 9:30.

"How much time do I have before you leave?", I asked Henry. He looked at the clock and said, "I plan on leaving between 11 and 11:30." I heard Laura's truck start. I then saw it go past the window.

"So, did you finish the box yet?", I questioned Henry.

"Yep, I plan on giving it to her later after the air show. I do this every time she finishes an air show at the festival. Sort of a tradition.", he revealed.

"Oh yeah?", I inquired.

"Yeah, I'm just grateful for when she gets back on the ground safe. She knows what she's doing but I always worry. When you're a parent, it's what happens.", he confided in me. I finished my last bite of ham.

"So what's the box for then?", I asked Henry. Henry stood up from the table. "Follow me. I'll show you.", he commanded.

I set the paper down on the table then stood up from the table and followed him. He exited the dining room and he went upstairs. I saw him open a door to a room on the right at the top of the stairs. I ascended the staircase and followed him into the room. I was blown away by what I saw.

There was a large diorama of Return on a very large table occupying most of the room. It had the enormous town square. I recognized the town sign, the town library, the town hall, the police station, the hospital, Lenny's, Martha's, the lighthouse, and even the farm. I also saw the clearing in the woods with the boulders. It reminded me of the model town from that movie, *Beetlejuice*.

"Wow. This is very cool. You made this?", I asked.

"Yep. Both Laura and I have been working on this for

years. Since she was a kid.", answered Henry. I looked at the diorama and noticed the area where the box was supposed to go. There was a small square hole in its place.

"I'm sure she's going to love it.", I affirmed. I looked at Henry and he formed a small grin. "Thanks.", he said.

"I'm envious of this. I wish I was I fortunate enough to have been involved in a project of this magnitude with my parents.", I admitted.

"Me too, Charlie. Me too.", Henry sympathized. He then added, "You might want to finish breakfast and get yourself ready. Close the door when you're done, please." He went back downstairs.

Yeah, he's right. I can marvel at this later.

I left the room and closed the door behind me. I headed back downstairs and finished my remaining breakfast. I heard Henry washing the dishes in the kitchen. After I cleared my plate, I brought it along with my utensils, the coffee mug, and the glass into the kitchen. I set them on the counter next to the Henry as I saw him washing a frying pan. "Thank you.", he said.

"No problem.", I told him. I went into the bathroom and got myself cleaned up for the day.

After that refreshing shower, I dried myself off, got dressed then walked into the laundry room and dropped the towel in the hamper.

I exited the house and headed back to the guest room in the barn. I entered the room and went into the bedroom to go through the clothes that Laura left me. There wasn't much of a wardrobe selection at my disposal hence I decided to stick with the jeans and boots I was still wearing. I changed my T-shirt but it was cooler than it had been the past few days so I opted to also wear the button-down shirt that was left for me.

    I finished getting dressed then exited the bedroom and closed the door. I walked out the door of the guest room as I also shut that door behind me. I saw Henry approaching his truck.

    "All set?", he asked.

    "I'm ready.", I confirmed. We both got in the truck. Henry started it up then turned up the volume of the rock and roll on the radio and pulled out of the driveway. We headed into town.

SIXTEEN

    Henry parked his truck on a side street off of the town square. The town square was blocked off with wooden traffic barriers and filled with lots of people. I would've guessed nearly every resident of the town had to have been occupying the square. We got out of the truck and walked towards the festival. We crossed the street and entered the wide open space. There was a small stage on the lawn of the square that had a group of guys playing bluegrass music. I saw various stands for food and other vendors showcasing their skills.
    I saw a caricature artist next to a hot dog stand. There was a woman selling jewelry near an ice cream truck. The

jewelry looked like it was personally made by her. I walked casually along with Henry. I noticed Derek with a red hat and a white apron using a barbeque smoker. He must've been making food for BBQ HQ. Next to him was another woman selling little plants in those small plastic containers. I walked up to Derek and Henry followed.

"Hello, Derek.", I said.

"Hey, Charlie! Here, it's on the house.", he enthusiastically greeted. He handed Henry and I each a cheeseburger slider.

"Thanks.", I replied.

"My pleasure. Enjoy and come back after you've looked around some more.", Derek said. He went back to using the smoker.

I bit into the slider and savored the bite.

Wow, this is so juicy and loaded with flavor. How does he do it?

I swallowed the food and ate the last morsel of my slider. Henry grabbed the paper plate from my hands as he already finished his slider and tossed both of our plates in a nearby trash can.

I looked around more of the area to take in the event. I also noticed the iron box. I saw a couple teenagers turning the dials on it. It seemed like they were trying to figure out the riddle.

"There she is.", observed Henry. He pointed towards the sky. I looked up and saw the blimp flying up there. There was a banner on the side of the blimp that read *The 200th Return Heritage Festival*. Along with the blimp were also a few hot air balloons floating up there with her.

"What a sight.", I said in amazement.

"It always is.", Henry agreed. I noticed more people heading towards the center of the square. There were some bleachers set up and people were taking seats on them. I looked at the clock on top of the town hall and it was noon.

"Looks like it should be starting very soon.", I said. Henry began to walk towards the center of the square where everyone was heading and I followed. I heard applause and then I heard a voice come out of a speaker in that direction.

"Good afternoon and welcome to the 200th Return Heritage Festival!", the voice announced. It sounded familiar but I couldn't place it. There were massive cheers coming from the crowd.

The voice continued on, "I would like to thank everyone in this town for making this festival what it is today and for getting this festival set up successfully for another year." The crowd was blocking me and I couldn't get a look at the speaker on the stage. More applause and cheering erupted from the crowd.

"We have many stands set up with a variety of vendors that span across food, beverages, arts, crafts, and other items that celebrate our town. There will also be the grand fireworks show later tonight. We're gonna kick things off with the air show so let's enjoy ourselves! We're here to have fun!", the voice concluded. Even louder applause and cheering was pouring out from the crowd. I finally got a look at the stage but the speaker had already left.

RETURN

"Here they come.", Henry said. I looked up and saw three fighter jets heading towards us. They passed right over us and flew above the blimp and the hot air balloons. The sound of the planes followed suit with a thundering whoosh. They came back around for another fly over and flew over us again.

After that maneuver, I saw the three jets increase their altitude and they turned around. They were flying back towards the square upside down and then flew over the town. Lots of people were cheering and clapping.

"Wow.", I praised.

"Oh yeah. These guys train a lot.", Henry affirmed.

The jets then split off in different directions and each one circled back towards the sky above us. The first jet passed between the hot air balloons from one direction and cleared them safely. The second jet repeated what the first one did but from the other direction. The third jet came in from another direction dodging the hot air balloons and also dodging the blimp. More applause and cheering ensued.

"Whoa. That's pretty dangerous.", I said to Henry.

Laura's okay. She's done this before.

"That's exactly why these guys train a lot. The blimp is old but that's Helium and not Hydrogen so don't worry about that.", replied Henry.

Hope she has a parachute.

I looked back at the sky and noticed a biplane entering the space occupied by the balloons and the blimp. The biplane circled them one time then pulled away. The biplane came back around and weaved in between the

balloons and the blimp. The crowd applauded again.
"Watch this.", Henry said.
I focused on the sky and the biplane came back around. It flew through the middle of a lane of hot air balloons. One fighter jet came from a direction perpendicular to the biplane's direction and crossed the path of the biplane. The jet and the biplane were close but did not make contact. A second fighter jet did the same thing and the third jet also did the same thing. The biplane cleared the path between the balloons and the crowd roared with applause and cheering.
"Oh, crap.", Henry fretted. I looked at him.
"What's wrong?" I asked.
"I just realized I left Laura's gift at the house. I always give it to her when she gets back on the ground. As soon as the show is over, which is not too much longer, she'll be landing the blimp.", Henry explained. I offered my help.
"I'll go back and get it for you. Don't worry. Where is it?", I volunteered. Henry took the keys to his truck out of his pocket and handed them to me.
"It's in the closet of the bedroom where you are currently sleeping. I hid it there because I didn't want Laura finding it in the house. It's in a small silver cardboard box.", Henry told me.
"Gotcha. I'll be back shortly.", I responded. I left Henry and the crowd as the planes continued to fly above everyone. I crossed the road to get back onto the side street. When I got to the other side, I saw Jack and he waved at me. I waved back.
"Where are you going? You're missing the show!",

RETURN

Jack remarked with surprise. "Yeah, I know. I'm helping Henry with something but I'll be back soon.", I explained. "Shake a leg! You don't want to miss the finale!", he said.

I walked away from Jack and made it towards the truck. I unlocked the door and got in. I started up the truck and carefully turned it around. I didn't want to hit any of the parked cars in the street. After finishing a five point turn, I got the truck in the right direction and headed towards the road back.

The drive back to the farm only took me a couple minutes. I pulled into the driveway then threw the truck in park and shut it off. I left the keys in the ignition and exited the truck.

I walked over to the barn and entered the guest room. The bedroom door was open, which I thought was strange, because I thought I closed it. I approached the closet and opened it. The small silver cardboard box stood out among the belongings on the top shelf inside. I took the box out of the closet and shut the door. I walked back to the door to exit the bedroom and a fist came around the corner and punched me in my left eye.

I fell backwards on to the bed, instantly reaching for my eye, and dropping the small silver box onto the floor. I looked up and saw Tyler standing in the doorway.

"Hello, Charlie.", he muttered.

That son of a bitch followed me in here and got the jump on me.

"Tyler, what the hell are you doing?", I complained in pain. He grabbed me by the shirt and punched my eye again. I fell back on the bed. My eye was throbbing. My head started to hurt again.

He grabbed me by the shirt again. His mouth was swollen and he had an angry look on his face. I think he was chewing tobacco. His breath smelled like shit.

"I'm making sure that you are not going to interfere with what I have to do. I'm skipping town and I'm taking Laura with me.", he said.

What an idiot. He's already violated his probation so he's going to escalate everything to kidnapping.

"Don't you think Laura has a say in this?", I told him.

He punched me in the stomach. The wind flew out of me. I was coughing and trying to catch my breath. He violently grabbed my hair and looked at me.

"I'm not going to let some city boy *faggot* take Laura from me. She's mine.", he added. He punched me in the side of the head. I was knocked back on to the bed. I saw the clock displaying as 1:01 on the nightstand. My head was radiating with pain and my vision was losing focus. I saw Tyler standing over me then he and the room faded into darkness.

SEVENTEEN

I woke up. I saw the room materialize. I didn't see Tyler. I looked at the clock. It was 1:22.

I've only been out for a little bit. I have to stop him.

I stood up from the bed. My head hurt like hell. My eye was throbbing with pulses of pain and felt like it was swelling to the size of a pomegranate. I didn't have time to look in a mirror.

I ran out of the bedroom and the guest room to get outside. I ran towards the driveway and I saw that Henry's truck was gone.

That bastard stole Henry's truck! How the hell am I going to catch Tyler? I looked at the barn.

No way. You are out of your damn mind.
I ran towards the barn and entered through the front. I ran over to Goliath's stable.

"Goliath!", I said. The horse looked at me and blew a heavy gust of air through his nose. I looked around and saw the saddle sitting on the table near by Goliath's stable. I grabbed the saddle and the bridle off of the table. Once I was able to hold both objects in my arms, I ran back over to Goliath's stable.

I need to get these on him.
"Goliath. I need your help, buddy. We have to save Laura!", I said.

Goliath neighed very loudly then stood on his hind legs and kicked open the stable door. It violently swung open but it did not come off the hinges. I was just out of the reach of the trajectory from that door. The door bounced once off of the stable and then lost momentum. Goliath walked out of the stable.

"Good boy.", I said.
Goliath huffed and puffed.
"Please help me out and stand still while I get these on you.", I pleaded with the horse. I put the saddle on his back and fastened it on to him. He was being cooperative.

After the saddle, I took the bridle and put it on Goliath's head. He very carefully put his mouth on the bit and was very obedient in letting me secure the bridle around his head. I hopped up on to the saddle and I was sitting right on top of Goliath.

What a good horse. I touched him gently on the mane. I

grabbed a hold of the reins attached to the bridle.

"Laura's in town and we need to save her! Let's go!", I yelled.

Goliath stood up on his hind legs and neighed with the intensity of a team of a hundred stallions. I held on with all my strength so I wouldn't fall off of him. He set all of his legs back down on the ground and then took off with a burst of speed towards the front exit of the barn. I ducked my head to ensure I wouldn't smack it on the frame of the front barn door on the way out. I sat back up after clearing the exit. He ran across the property towards the road and rushed in the direction of the town square.

This horse is fast!

I was just flying by all the houses on the road and holding on for dear life. I was focusing on how the hell I was going to stop Tyler. I had no idea what he was going to do. I had no idea what I was going to do. Tyler had a head start on me. I needed to find Laura. I needed to find Henry. I needed to find Jack.

Goliath was quickly approaching the wooden barrier on the road that was blocking traffic from the town square. I tugged on the reins and yelled "Whoa!" The horse slowed down then stopped. I dismounted from the horse and tied up his reins to a nearby light post.

I looked at Goliath. "Sorry, buddy. Laura would kill me if I lost you.", I said to the horse. Goliath just blew hard through his nose.

I ran across the street and into the town square. As I

was closing in on the center of the festival, I noticed that the blimp had landed. I looked closer and I saw Laura standing in front of it. I also saw Tyler holding her by the arm and then he started to force her into entering the gondola.

"Laura!", I yelled.

Both of them entered the gondola. I started to make my way through the crowd as fast as I could and it seemed like every resident in this town was getting in my way.

I heard a loud motor start up. I realized it was the blimp. I picked up my pace and just started pushing people out of the way. Some lady with kids called me a jerk. I heard other people calling out their grievances with me rudely cutting through them.

Suddenly, I felt a big hand on my shoulder. It was Henry.

"Charlie, what the hell are you doing and what the hell happened to you?", he asked me.

"Tyler did this.", I said in a panic. "He's also got Laura in the blimp and he's taking her away." Henry instantly let go of me and he looked at the blimp. We both saw that it was starting to go up.

"Oh, shit.", he said. "We gotta stop him. Go!"

I ran with fire on my heels after the blimp and sprinted ahead of Henry. I finally got close to the landing zone and saw a rope hanging from the rear of the cabin attached to the aircraft.

Don't you think of jumping up there.

I jumped up and grabbed the rope. The blimp was moving further away from the ground much quickly than I anticipated. I clenched onto the rope as tightly as I could.

"Charlie! Are you nuts?!", yelled Henry from the ground below.

I was a little too frightened to say something back. I came to the realization that I'm hanging on to a rope above a crowd of strangers and if I fell, I wasn't going to survive.

"Oh, Charlie. What the hell are you doing up here?", I said to myself in a petrified manner.

Then I thought about Laura.

I can't let that asshole take her away from me, from Henry, from her own life here. Who knows what the hell he would do? He is dangerous.

I wrapped my leg around the rope to shift my weight and started to climb. One hand over the other and I was slowly making progress towards reaching the blimp. I felt sweat coming off my brow and I made the mistake of looking down.

Oh, shit.

I saw the whole town square now. I looked back up at the blimp.

Only another few feet and I'll be there. I reached up again and pulled myself closer.

One more grab on the rope to pull myself upward and I should be able to reach the door of the gondola. I grabbed the next section of rope above me and pulled myself closer.

I took my left arm and wrapped it around the rope to get a better grip. Once I had got that situated, I reached for the door of the cabin and grabbed the handle. I was tugging downward on the handle and the door flew open. I reached into the cabin and with a heavy groan, I pulled myself into the cabin and laid on the floor for a moment to collect myself.

    I stood up from the floor of the cabin and the wind was blowing through the open door and into my face.

    "Stop right there! Why can't you just go away?!", Tyler yelled.

    I looked up and saw that he had a revolver pointed at me. I couldn't tell exactly what caliber it was. It might have been a .38. I saw Laura at the controls of the blimp and she was staring back at me with a frightened look on her face.

    "I could say the same thing to you, Tyler!", I began. "Why are you doing this?!"

    "Laura is leaving with me! I'm not going back to jail and I'm not going to be without her!", he hollered.

    "All you had was a parole violation. Now, you've just added kidnapping, assault, and grand larceny to your list. If that gun goes off, it'll be much worse for you.", I said back.

    "That's why I have the gun! I know what the stakes are and no one is going to stop me! She is mine!", Tyler yelled at me. I saw Laura shake her head but I could tell she was still frightened. I was starting to lose my cool.

    "Oh yeah?! She's yours?! You just had to force her into the blimp and then she'll come around and you guys will live happily ever after?! Wake up, Tyler! If she was truly yours, we wouldn't be in this situation! You wouldn't be wanted by the police! Laura wouldn't be frightened! I wouldn't have climbed a rope high above the town to be in this blimp with a gun in my face! I'm sick of this bullshit

AND MY HEAD FUCKING HURTS!!", I screamed.

"Who cares about you or what you think!", Tyler snapped.

"I do."

I saw Laura's boot swing through between Tyler's legs from behind and kick him in the crotch. Tyler went down on his knees and shrieked in pain.

"That's for trying to stab Charlie *and* my father, you psycho!", Laura said.

I ran over to Tyler and tried to wrestle the gun away from him but Tyler was not letting go easily. In the struggle, both of us had the gun pointed towards the controls of the blimp. Laura ducked out of the way and the gun went off. The bullet hit the control panel and the blimp shook. I kept wrestling with his arm and the gun was now pointed towards the ceiling of the gondola. The revolver went off again and the bullet went through the ceiling. The blimp began tilting right and left.

The new turbulence shifted the cabin and knocked Tyler and I towards the rear of the gondola as we crashed onto the floor. The gun flew out of our hands and started sliding around the floor. Laura tumbled towards the open door and screamed as half of her was suddenly hanging outside from the blimp. She was holding on to the cabin and the door.

"Laura!", I yelled.

"Charlie!", she yelled back.

Tyler grabbed my shoulder and my immediate reaction was punching him as hard as I could in the face. I felt his nose break. He grabbed for his nose as blood started dripping out of his nostrils and tears welled up in his eyes. I rushed over to Laura and dove at her to grab her. I grasped on to her right arm and wrapped my other arm around her torso.

"Grab on to me!", I commanded. I felt her reach around my back and squeeze as I began to pull her back in to the blimp. When I got a significant portion of her back inside, I gripped on to her belt and pulled her legs back in to the cabin. I closed the door shut and then hugged Laura. She hugged me back.

"Are you okay?", I asked her.

"Yeah, I'm okay but I got to get to the controls.", she said. She got on her hands and knees, quickly crawled around the seats and across the floor then made her way back to the pilot's seat as the cabin kept shaking. She sat back in the chair and buckled her seat belt. She flicked off a switch, maintained control of the rudders, rolled the elevator wheel and leveled the blimp. It was flying straight again but it was starting to make alarming sounds.

"What about Tyler?", I pondered. I looked back at him and saw that he was still conscious but wincing in pain. I saw Laura reach into a tool box and she pulled out a roll of duct tape. She looked at me with a smirk.

"Pfft... duct tape.", I said. I took the roll from her and began to unravel it. During the turbulence, I made my way over to Tyler, grabbed one of his wrists and began to tie it to the other one. I wrapped multiple layers of tape around his wrists and then tore the tape from the roll.

I ventured back over to Laura and put the roll back in the tool box. She was flicking switches and looking at her gauges.

"Oh no, we're losing pressure in the envelope.", she acknowledged. I sat down in the seat next to her. I realized that now we were over the farm. She was descending in her approach towards an open field past her house near the lake.

"Buckle up!", she demanded. I grabbed my belt and fastened myself into the seat. She opened up the landing gear. She seemed to be coming in a little fast. She was holding tightly on to the throttle and trying to ease it up. She was pedaling frantically on the rudders and turning the wheel. "Come on, come on, you old piece of shit!", she shouted. She got the blimp out of a nose dive and then we crashed into the dirt. We both jerked forward on impact and Tyler slid into the backs of our seats. The gondola was sliding along and we saw the edge of the cliff coming up. We were slowing down but the edge of the cliff was getting closer. She put the throttle all the way down and she killed the engine. The gondola was sliding still and then it finally came to a halt.

We were back on the ground and we were looking at the lake. There was still a few yards of land between us and the edge but we were still a little too close for comfort.

I looked at Laura and she looked at me and nodded. Police sirens started getting closer. We both let out a collective sigh of relief. I saw Tyler on the ground behind us.

He appeared to be unconscious but he was still breathing.
Nobody died. Thank God. Even though, I wasn't one to usually give him praise.

There was a knock on the door of the cabin. It was Jack.

"Charlie! Laura!", Jack yelled.

"Yeah, we're okay!", I yelled back. I got up from the seat, stepped over Tyler and opened the door. Jack walked in and he saw the gun laying against the back of one of the seats.

"Whose gun is this?", asked Jack.

"It's Tyler's. He just threatened the both of us with it.", explained Laura. Jack looked over at Tyler, who seemed to be regaining consciousness, and saw him tied up with the duct tape and blood running down his face. Jack went over to Tyler and Jack cracked a smirk. Jack turned Tyler onto his back and he put his foot on Tyler's shoulder.

"Well, Tyler.", Jack started. "Kidnapping. Assault. Unlawful possession of a firearm. Aircraft Hijacking, which is a felony I might add. I've now got more stuff to keep you in jail for a while. You're under arrest."

EIGHTEEN

I saw Jack escort a handcuffed Tyler with a bandage covering his broken nose to the police cruiser. He opened the back door and Tyler willingly entered the back. I was a little surprised by the cooperation. He probably figured he should cooperate considering the shit storm he's caused.

Laura and I were sitting in the back of an ambulance with the door wide open. There was an EMT checking out Laura and I for any injuries. Laura seemed fine and I was dealing with the pain in my head and eye. The medic that was focused on me was cleaning up my wounds.

"Your eye will probably swell up but if you take some

Ibuprofen and use a cold compress that should help reduce the swelling.", she suggested.

"Thanks.", I said to the medic. I turned to Laura. "How are you?", I asked her.

"I still got my adrenaline going a bit and I'm trying to calm down. Other than that, I'm okay.", she responded. "How about you?", she asked me.

"Same.", I nodded with a smile. Laura grabbed my hand and looked at me in a new way. It was a look of compassion and seemed to be one where she expressed how deeply she cared for me. I've seen Heidi give me a similar look before.

Heidi is not around anymore. She does not want you. Laura is here with you now. Focus on her.

"My head hurts like hell though.", I admitted. Laura smiled and said "Don't worry, babe. I'm your nurse. I'll take care of ya." We saw lights pull into the driveway. It was Henry's truck. He pulled in front of the garage and parked the truck. He turned it off and ran over to us.

"Are you two alright?", he asked.

"We're fine, Dad.", Laura said.

"I see you found your truck. Tyler stole it from me when I was here.", I said.

Henry was bewildered. "That jerk touched my truck? Well, at least he wasn't smart enough to take it far away. I found it in the exact same spot where we parked. The keys were in the ignition." Both Laura and I chuckled.

"Oh, crap.", I said. "I just remembered. In order to try and stop Tyler, I took Goliath out of the barn and rode him into town." Laura was shocked.

"You rode Goliath?", she inquired.

"Don't worry. I tied him to a light post so he wouldn't take off. I'm sorry that I took him.", I added.

"Well, considering the circumstances, it's okay. I forgive you.", Laura reasoned. Laura reached into her pocket and pulled out a set of keys. She gave the keys to Henry.

"Dad, could you please go get my truck? It is parked in the parking lot behind the Town Library. I'll go into town and bring Goliath home.", Laura said. "No problem, sweetie. I'll see you when you get back.", said Henry.

He walked away from us and signaled Jack. Jack acknowledged him and Henry got in the front seat of the police cruiser. The cruiser started up and ventured into town.

I got up from my seat in the ambulance and stepped out onto the pavement. Laura followed suit. I was thankful that both Laura and I were standing on our feet. It was becoming overwhelming still trying to shake off the feeling of adrenaline pumping through me. I hugged Laura and she tightly hugged me back. We looked at the field near the edge of the cliff and saw the wreckage of the blimp.

"What about that?", I wondered as I pointed to the wreckage. Laura looked and said, "I'm sure they will just wait until tomorrow to clean it up. At least it's not on fire." I nodded in agreement and we broke contact from the hug.

"Hey, you were amazing in the blimp.", I told Laura. She chuckled.

"Thanks but maybe Dad is right. It might be time to

scrap that old flying windbag of nuts and bolts.", she confided in me.

"So, should we go get Goliath then?", I asked Laura. "Yeah", she agreed, "but let's get a ride into town." Laura looked at one of the paramedics and pleaded, "Could you guys please give us a ride to the town square?"

"No problem. Get in the back.", the paramedic answered. We hopped back into the ambulance and closed the doors. We sat down next to each other. The ambulance backed up and began to beep. I put my arm around Laura and she held on to me. The paramedic moved the ambulance next to Henry's truck. She put the truck in drive and exited the driveway.

I could feel the lead foot on the paramedic. It seemed like we were going extremely fast. I tried to lighten things up.

"I got to see part of the air show. It was very cool. You were great.", I complimented. Laura looked at me and smiled. "All I did was fly the blimp. The pilots who flew the jets and that biplane are the skilled ones.", she noted.

"Don't be so modest. I can't fly.", I said and then I gave her a small kiss on the lips. She smiled at me and whispered, "Thank you. You're pretty great." That warmed my heart. I felt the ambulance slowing down and then it came to a stop.

"We're here. I'm guessing that's your horse?" uttered the paramedic. "I hope so.", Laura spoke. We both got up and exited out of the back doors. "Thank you!", I said back to the paramedic. She stuck her hand out of the window and waved. I closed the door. The ambulance drove on as the wooden traffic barrier was gone. We walked over to the light post and Goliath was still there.

He saw Laura and greeted her with a boisterous neigh. Laura walked over to him and gave him a hug. "My baby boy! C'mon, let's get you home." She untied the reigns from the post and hopped on to the horse in one swift movement. She reached her hand out to me.

"Come on. Hop on back.", she commanded. I grabbed her hand and used the outside of the stirrup as a boost. I pushed myself up and with the assistance of Laura, I was on top of the horse and sitting behind Laura.

"Put your arms around me and hold on tight.", she instructed. I put my arms around her waist. "Ready?", she asked. "Yep", I responded.

"Walk.", she commanded. Goliath began to trot at a steady pace down the road back to the farm. I was bouncing on the back as Laura was controlling the beast below us. The lights of the town were fading away behind us and the moonlight was starting to overcome our environment. I looked up at the sky and it was another clear night littered with dozens of stars.

"It's such a beautiful night.", Laura observed.

"It doesn't compare to how beautiful you are.", I told her. I felt her grab my hand. I saw the farm coming into view.

"All you need now is a Stetson and you'll be a full-on

cowgirl.", I remarked. Laura chuckled. "I have a few but they're at the house.", she replied. "I bet they look great on you.", I reassured her.

Laura's truck pulled up to us and rode next to us. Henry yelled out the window, "Hey, after you put Goliath away come into the house. I have to talk to both of you."

"Okay.", said Laura. Henry drove on ahead and I saw him pull into their driveway. Henry parked it next to his truck. He got out of the truck as soon as we were walking up to the property line of the farm and I saw him head towards the guest room. Goliath walked up to the front entrance of barn.

"Whoa.", commanded Laura. Goliath stopped. I hopped off the horse first and then Laura dismounted. She grabbed him by the reins and said, "I'll be inside in a couple minutes. You go ahead." I nodded and I pet Goliath on the head.

"See you later, buddy.", I said to Goliath. Goliath nickered. I walked towards the house. Laura walked Goliath back into the barn. As I was nearing the garage, I noticed Henry behind me walking away from the barn, holding the silver box with Laura's gift. I stopped and looked at him.

"I see you found the box. Sorry about that. I must've dropped that when Tyler caught me off guard."

"Don't worry about it, Charlie. How's the head?", Henry asked.

"Been better but I'll get by.", I told him.

"Good.", he responded. He put a hand on my shoulder. "Come on, let's get inside. I got a little something that'll take the edge off.", he assured me. I followed him into the house and I saw him go into the dining room and turn on the lights. "Come in here and have a seat.", he advised. I walked into the dining room and sat down at the table. Henry walked over to the liquor cabinet and opened it. He pulled out a bottle of whiskey and set it on the table along with the silver box. He went back to the cabinet and also took out three glasses. He set them on the table.

"I only bring this whiskey out on special occasions.", revealed Henry. I heard the front door open and Laura walked into the dining room. She noticed the whiskey and the glasses.

"Oh, you brought out the whiskey? What for?", she asked.

"It's a special occasion so I brought out the special whiskey.", stated Henry. I picked up the bottle and noticed a date stamped on it.

March 11 1984.

"Wow, this whiskey is older than I am.", I said. I set the bottle down and Henry picked it up. He opened the bottle and poured a finger into each glass. He set the bottle down and closed it. He picked up two glasses then gave one to me and the other to Laura. Henry picked up the remaining glass and raised it.

"To my wonderful daughter on another successful year at the festival. And... to Charlie for helping her when she was in danger. And... to that asshole going to jail for a while.", he toasted. He took a sip of the whiskey and Laura and I did the same. It was incredibly smooth and there was a slow burn traveling down my esophagus and into my stomach.

"Damn, that was fantastic. Thanks.", I commented. Henry smiled.

"You're welcome, Charlie.", said Henry. He picked up the bottle of whiskey, put it back in the cabinet then closed the cabinet.

"Dad," started Laura. "Charlie did more than help me. He saved my life." Henry was shocked and he looked at me.

"Well I had to. I care about her. Plus, Laura saved everyone on the blimp. She's the hero.", I humbly admitted.

"Yeah, but if you hadn't saved me from falling out of the blimp, I wouldn't have been able to save us.", she corrected me.

I didn't think about it like that but she was right. If I didn't save her, I'd probably be dead too.

Henry set his glass down on the table and he hugged me. "Thank you for saving my daughter's life.", Henry praised. He let go of me.

"It's no problem. You're welcome.", I replied back. Henry finished the rest of his whiskey and gazed at his empty glass with great satisfaction. Laura and I also finished our glasses. Henry set his empty glass on the table then grabbed the small silver box and handed it to Laura.

"For you, Sweetie.", he said.

"Oh? What's in here?", Laura asked. She opened the silver box and it was the completed replica of the box that

Henry created. It was even painted like the box and had the dials.

"Dad! This is so cool." She began to analyze the miniature replica. "You made this look real nice. It'll look great with the diorama.", approved Laura. She exited the room and headed upstairs. Henry and I followed her. She entered the room with the diorama and as soon as I walked in the doorway, I saw her place the miniature replica in the small hollow that was waiting for it.

"Have you seen this yet?", Laura asked me.

"Yeah, Henry showed this to me this morning actually after you left. It's very cool." Henry walked in behind me and Laura went up to him and hugged him.

"Thanks, Dad. I love you.", she beamed.

"I love you too, Sweetie.", said Henry. They stopped hugging and Henry made his way to the door then said, "Alright, I've had enough excitement for one day. Get the lights when you're done. I'm hitting the hay. Good night, you two."

"Good night, Dad."

"Good night, Henry." Henry walked out of the room and down the hall. I heard a door close. Laura looked at me.

"Let's go to my room real quick. I'll show you the Stetsons I have.", she said. She winked at me and I chuckled. I walked out the door then she turned off the light and closed the door behind us. She walked ahead of me then I followed her down the hall to a room and we entered it.

Her bedroom looked very nice. The walls were blue and she had a queen size bed. She had a wooden dresser adorned with brass handles along with a huge round mirror. There was a small pile of books sitting on top of the dresser. Next to the dresser was a plant with big green leaves in a large ceramic pot sitting on the ground in front of the window. Above the plant was a rack with three Stetson hats hanging from it.

"It's getting a little chilly out and the night is still young. Which one do you like? White, black or brown?", she asked.

"My vote is for white.", I decided.

"I like your style.", she agreed. She picked the white Stetson off of the rack and put it on her head. She looked in the mirror and adjusted it accordingly.

"Yep. Just like I thought. It looks great on you.", I reassured her. Laura smiled then turned around and kissed me on the lips. She went back over to the rack and put the black Stetson on me.

"Well, well. You're a fine looking cowboy.", she said. I smiled at her and then looked in the mirror. I stared for a couple moments and I agreed with her. I didn't look so bad with the hat on.

"You're right. Even with the bruised eye, it's not a bad look. I look like the bad guy in a Western movie.", I joked. She laughed. I opted to take the hat off and I put it back on the rack. I went back over to Laura and grabbed her around the waist.

"So, what do you want to do?", she asked me.

I had no idea. I just had a strong urge to be with her.

"Well, let's get out of the house and we'll just wing

it.", I offered. Laura kissed me again and then said, "It's a date."

NINETEEN

We walked out of the house and Laura closed the door behind us. The sun had gone completely down and night had unfolded. I followed her over to the garage and we entered through the side door. She walked up to the refrigerator that was on the opposite end. She opened it up then pulled out two beers and handed me one. I cracked mine open and then she opened hers.

"Cheers.", Laura said and I knocked cans with her. We sipped our beers and I found the cold frothy goodness to be very refreshing. Laura closed the refrigerator and took a blanket from the top of the refrigerator. She tucked it underneath her arm. We walked back outside and she closed the side door behind us.

We held hands and walked towards the direction of the lake. The view was absolutely breathtaking even with the wreckage of the blimp sitting at the edge of the cliff. The stars were reflecting off the surface of the water. We stopped and she laid the blanket down on the ground. We sat down on top of it. I loved how the moonlight was shining off of her.

"Before I forget, have you heard from my uncle at all lately?", I asked.

"No, he hasn't called or left any messages. I'm sure he'll get back to us soon.", she answered. I nodded and took a sip of my beer.

"It's quite beautiful where you live. Every part of nature I've seen since I've been here has been unlike anything I've seen.", I admitted.

"Yeah, it's home. I can't imagine myself being anywhere else.", Laura agreed. She took a sip of her beer. I was thinking about us and I wanted to ask her.

You know what? I'm going to ask her. I've been here for a week now and even though it's gone by fast, we've been through a lot already together.

"Laura...", I started. She looked at me with full attention and then the words came out.

"So, what is this that we have here?", I questioned her. She seemed confused when I said that.

"What do you think we have here?", she asked back.

"Well, I would like to think that this could be a

meaningful long-term relationship. We've been through so much over these past few days and I can't ignore the chemistry we have between each other. I want us to be together." She smiled and kissed me.

"I want that, too.", she approved.

So far so good.

"So I could call you my girlfriend and you're okay with that?", I asked.

"Well, what about Heidi? Is that over for good?"

"Heidi doesn't want to be in my life anymore and I have to move on. You're here with me now and not her. So, yes. That is over for good."

"If that is the case, then I'm more than okay with being your girlfriend if I can call you my boyfriend."

"I'm more than okay with that. You're my girlfriend."

"And you're my boyfriend. We're a couple." We kissed and locked our lips for a few moments. We looked at each other.

"Well, what if I moved here?", I asked. Laura's eyes lit up like a child's on Christmas. "Would you really move here for me?", she cheerfully asked.

I thought about it.

Heidi was not in my life anymore. Laura was now my girlfriend. I don't have a job. I don't have a car. I'm not extremely far from my Uncle Greg. I could always visit or he could come out here and meet Laura and Henry. I really like it here. It is so different and relaxing out here. I no longer have to deal with some prick trying to break up my girlfriend and I, both back there and here.

RETURN

I couldn't think of a reason not to live out here.

"Yes. Yes, I would.", I confessed. Laura kissed me.

"Alright, you can stay with me.", she said. I saw the sky light up with a flash of pink. We both turned around and saw fireworks shooting up into the sky from the direction of the town. It was an exploding canvas of rainbow colored lights that illuminated the sky. I took that as a good sign. I kissed her back and held her head as I continued to smooch her. The kissing stopped and then she hugged me.

"You know. It's colder than I thought. Let's go inside.", she suggested.

"Lead the way.", I said. We stood up from the blanket. Laura picked it up off the ground and carried the lumped up blanket under her arm. She held my hand and we walked back to the barn as the fireworks kept decorating the atmosphere above us. I finished off my beer. Laura finished her last sip then crushed the can. I took the can from her.

She opened the door of the guest room and walked inside. I followed her inside and she closed the door behind me. I dropped the two cans into the trash. She walked into the bedroom and asked "Do you need anything else tonight before bed?"

All I thought was yeah.

Her.

I walked into the bedroom and she closed the door behind me. She got very close to me and grabbed my head then stuck her tongue in my mouth. She was passionately kissing me and I kissed her back with intense ardor. She grabbed my butt and I grabbed hers. I broke away from her lips and softly kissed her neck. I heard her breathing become more heavy. I stopped the kissing.

I looked into her eyes and I said, "I want you."

"I want you so bad.", she told me.

I gently grabbed her crotch and I felt a shiver go through her. I could feel a slight dampness beneath the denim.

"You like that?", I asked her.

"Yes. Keep touching me there.", she pleaded. I was rubbing her there and she let out a quiet moan. I took her hand and put it on my erection poking from the front of my jeans. She let out a small shriek.

"I like it when you touch me there.", I told her. I took my hand and stuck it down the front of her jeans. I was sensually massaging the lips of her vagina and I stuck a finger in her. She gasped and I saw her knees buckle. I could feel how moist she was and saw her yearning for my member. Then I remembered that Laura told me that she likes dirty talk.

"I want to put my cock in your pussy." Laura shrieked again.

"Oh, say that again.", Laura begged.

"I want to put my cock in your pussy. Do you want that?"

"Yes, I want that! Put your cock in my pussy!" She pushed me and I fell backwards onto the bed. She jumped on top of me and kissed me hard. She started to undo my belt and open my jeans. I began to undo her belt. I unbuttoned her jeans then pulled down the zipper. She reached for my cock and started stroking it.

"You like that, my sexy cowboy?", she seductively asked.

"Yeah, I like that."

"How about this?", she asked. She took me in her mouth and I saw her head move up and down. I don't know what she was doing with the tongue but it was incredible. I cried out in pleasure. She stopped doing it. I took her and eased her off of me and onto the bed. She laid down and I got on top of her. I looked her in the eyes.

"Oh, yeah. Take me.", she insisted.

"You want me inside you?", I asked her.

"Yes, please. Fuck me, Charlie.", she begged.

I pulled her jeans down around her perfect ass then lifted her legs in the air and over my shoulders. I inserted myself in her and she inhaled with a sharp gasp. I felt myself expand within her warm and wet womanhood. I grabbed on to her bare ass and I felt her tremble. I thrusted and she let out a howl of ecstasy. I thrusted again and she howled even louder.

TWENTY

I woke up. I was naked. Laura was cuddling with me as she was asleep and she was also naked. I saw that the sun was coming up. I looked at her. She looked so peaceful.
She is so beautiful and I'm madly in love with her.
I gave her a small kiss on the lips and I saw her eyes open. She was staring into my eyes and smiling.
"Good morning, Handsome."
"Good morning, Gorgeous."
She kissed me. "Last night was incredible. I slept so well.", Laura said. "I loved it when you were on top while wearing the hat. I was completely into it.", I admitted to Laura. She smiled. "I can't believe you went three times.

Where do you get the energy?", she joked.

I think I felt myself blushing. I chuckled but I tried to be humble. The whole night here in the bedroom felt like a blur.

"I don't know. I guess I just wanted you that badly.", I said.

"You got me, Cowboy." Laura leaned into me and kissed me again. She slowly pulled away from my lips and cuddled with me. I looked up at the ceiling staring at nothing in particular. I was just relishing this very moment as much as I could.

"So what's the plan for today?", Laura asked.

"Not sure. I'm just following your lead.", I conceded. Laura turned her head and looked in my eyes.

"Well... how about we stay in bed for a little bit? Maybe fool around again. Then we'll have breakfast and we'll go from there."

"Sounds like a plan."

We softly kissed each other. I looked into her eyes.

"I love how I feel when I'm with you. I haven't felt so at home in so long.", I confessed to Laura. She gently kissed me.

"I'm glad you feel that way.", she approved. She held my head and looked into my eyes.

"This farm is my home and always will be. This town, the lighthouse and the lake. It's all a part of who I am and I wouldn't want to be anywhere else with anyone else. I want you to stay with me here. I want you to be in my life.", she added. I kissed her.

"I want to stay here with you. I'm not going anywhere. I want to be a part of your life and I want you to be part of mine.", I told her.

I love her.
Don't say that yet.
Wait a minute. What did she just say?
The lake.

"The lake?", I said.

"What?", said Laura.

I think I just had a breakthrough with the riddle. I sat up then stood up from the bed and picked my clothes up from the floor. I put them on in a hurry and began to put on my boots. Laura sat up in bed.

"Charlie? What's going on?", Laura asked me.

"The lake is north of us.", I stated. Laura seemed flummoxed by this statement.

"Yeah, so?", she acknowledged. She sounded unimpressed. I looked at her and I recited, "Find true north and you will find your way home."

She got out of bed and started getting dressed. I opened the door and walked out of the bedroom. I exited the guest room and went outside. The deflated wreckage of the crashed blimp was still sitting at the edge of the cliff.

I turned the corner and walked across the property towards the direction of the path in the woods. I heard the guest door open behind me and looked back to see Laura fully clothed and running after me.

"Charlie!", she yelled. I heard her but I kept walking towards the woods. I needed to know if this revelation I just had was correct or not.

RETURN

I entered the path dodging various branches and avoiding mud pits. Footsteps were hitting the trail and branches were rustling as I heard Laura enter the path behind me.

"Charlie! Where are you going?!", she shouted at me from afar. I kept walking down the path and she followed me.

I was nearing the end of the path and I finally got to the clearing. I stopped and looked at the arrangement of boulders. I heard Laura coming up from behind. She walked out of the path and stood next to me. She was looking at the arrangement.

"Okay, Doctor Jones, did you find the ark? What are we doing out here?", she asked me.

I stuck out my left arm and pointed to my left.

"North is that way, correct?" Laura looked at me.

"Yes, north is that way.", Laura answered. I started walking to the right side of arrangement in order to face north. I began telling Laura what I was thinking.

"The name of this painting is called 'The Beginning and The End.' Sounds like a completion of a cycle to me. These numbers are the basis of the universe." I got to the right side of the clearing and stopped walking. I turned and faced north. I was simultaneously dumbfounded and amazed.

A one and a zero.
10
"Ten.", I pointed out.
Laura saw it too then said, "Holy shit."

I nodded in agreement. "I got a hunch that this has to be part of the code to unlock the box.", I guessed. From this position, I also realized something else with the arrangement.

"Look at that. The one is made up of ten boulders and the zero is also made up of ten boulders.", I stated. I saw Laura counting out the boulders and then she said, "What the hell?"

I heard some movement from the path and we both saw Henry exit from the path and enter the clearing.

"What are you two yelling about so early this morning?", Henry asked. For an old man, he had the ears of a hawk hunting for prey.

"Dad, come look at this!", said Laura with amazement. Henry walked over to where we were and we had him look at the boulders from our point of view. Henry's jaw dropped.

"How have I not noticed this before? It's the number ten!", Henry observed.

"Yeah, my money is on this being the first two numbers for the code on the box.", I theorized.

"Could it really be that simple?", questioned Laura. Henry looked at both of us and said, "Let's go find out."

TWENTY-ONE

Henry drove into town with Laura and I accompanying him in his truck. He entered into the town square and pulled up next to the town library. He parked the truck and turned the engine off. The stands and the rides were still set up in the square but there were no visible occupants.

Laura, Henry and I exited the truck and we crossed the street to get to the square. I brought my pace to a mild jog, as I was feeling very excited about the notion of figuring this out, and approached the box. I looked at the plinth to read the riddle again.

THIS IS THE KEY TO THE UNIVERSE.

FIGURE OUT THE CODE AND YOU WILL POSSESS IT.

FIND TRUE NORTH AND YOU WILL FIND YOUR WAY HOME.

1. The first two numbers are the basis of the universe when separated but together they are a completion of a cycle.

2. The next two numbers are the antithesis of 1.

3. A hundred score will give you four numbers, but take away the sum of the first two pairs and you will get the last two pairs.

Laura and Henry walked up behind me and Laura began to read the riddle out loud. I touched the first dial and scrolled it until it displayed a 1. Then I scrolled the second dial until it was displaying a 0. Nothing happened with the box.
"Okay. So what are the other numbers?", Laura questioned. I was thinking about it and I wasn't really sure.
"Well, what's the antithesis of one?", asked Henry.
"I'm not sure. I'd say negative one but that wouldn't make sense because there's no minus symbol on any of the dials.", I stated. I was thinking about it some more and I couldn't come up with anything. I read the riddle again.

RETURN

Something in the riddle jumped out at me.

1 but not one.

"Hmm.", I curiously said.

"What? What is it?", asked Laura.

"Well, something about the riddle with the clues. Maybe it's a stretch but maybe it's not.", I commented.

"Like what?", inquired Henry. I decided to talk it out loud and get their input.

"I'm assuming because it is a riddle that these clues on the plinth are supposed to lead to us figuring out what the code is, right?"

"I would hope so if this were a normal riddle.", retorted Henry.

"So, I'm reading this again and I noticed that every time a number is mentioned in the riddle that it is spelled out except for at the end of clue two. Why?", I pointed out. Laura and Henry both looked at the riddle.

"Okay, I see what you're saying but why would that be important?", Laura rebutted.

"I'm not sure but putting the actual number in the riddle instead of spelling it out like the rest of the numbers. Two, two, a hundred, four, two, two. It seems out of place.", I explained. I thought it about it some more as I was pacing around the box.

Henry got closer to the box and stared at the dials. He looked back at the riddle then went back to looking at the box. I looked at the riddle again and Laura looked with me.

"The antithesis of 1.", I said aloud. Then it hit me.

"Wait.", I blurted out. Henry and Laura looked at me. I continued on with my thought process. "What if the riddle is not referring to the number one but clue one?", I proposed to them.

Both of their eyes widened with discovery.

"So... if that's the case then what's the antithesis of 10?", she asked.

I walked over to the box. I scrolled the third dial until it displayed a 0. After I selected that number, I scrolled the fourth dial until it displayed a 1. Nothing seemed to happen with the box.

Henry was analyzing the entire box and he shook his head. "Nothing.", he concluded.

I read clue three of the riddle again. I decided to start with what we possibly did know.

"Okay, so in reading clue three. The sum of the first two pairs would be 11, assuming that these numbers are right, correct?", I asked them.

"Yes.", confirmed Laura and Henry.

"So how does 11 get us the last four numbers? A hundred is not four numbers either. If I subtract 11 from 100, I just get two numbers. Even if I add 11 to 100, I do not get four numbers. I get three.", I thought out loud.

I paced around the box again thinking about those numbers. 100. 11. 2. 2. 4. 2. 2. 10. 1. I was trying to think of possible combinations but it wasn't making sense with what I had. I wasn't even completely sure that the numbers I had so far were correct. Something had to be missing from this that I wasn't seeing. Adding all these numbers up would not give me eight digits and putting the numbers together would not give me eight digits either.

RETURN

What am I not seeing here?

"A hundred score will give you four numbers.", I repeated.

"A hundred points?", Laura guessed. She looked bewildered. I looked at the plinth and read the clue again and said, "I don't know."

I looked up and back at the both of them. Laura was rubbing her cheek and seemed deep in thought. Henry was just staring at the box and maybe hoping the answer would just jump out at him.

"One hundred score.", said Henry. "One hundred *score*.", he said again but with more enthusiasm.

"What's on your mind, Henry?", I asked him.

"Score is a number!", Henry exclaimed. I wasn't getting it at first then Henry said "Lincoln's famous speech." Then that realization just hit me and Laura.

"Oh, you're right. A score is twenty!", I affirmed.

"One hundred times twenty is...", Laura said.

"Two thousand. Four numbers." I proudly surmised.

"If you take away eleven, then you get...", Laura said.

I reached over to the fifth dial and scrolled it until a 1 was displaying. I went to the sixth dial and entered a 9. Next, I went to the seventh dial and scrolled that one so it displayed as 8. Lastly, I scrolled the eighth dial to display a 9. I heard some mechanical motion occurring inside the box.

The circular section on top of the box opened. We all took step back due to our unexpected surprise. I looked at the code and I was a little freaked out.

10011989

"That is really bizarre.", I remarked.

"Why is that bizarre?", asked Laura.

"Ten zero one, nineteen eighty-nine. That's my birthday.", I announced. Laura's eyes grew wide with shock. I slowly took a step forward and looked inside the box. It was surprisingly dark inside there and I couldn't really make out what was in there.

"I can't see in there.", I noted.

"Come on kid, you've gone too far now to not find out what's in there. Reach in.", said Henry. I looked at Henry and I knew he was right.

I was anxious and I reached in the box. The hollow inside was very narrow and I was just able to fit my hand in there. I felt something. It seemed dowel shaped and made of glass. It almost seemed like a test tube that was used in labs. I got a grip on the object and pulled it out of the box carefully.

It was a glass tube with a cork sealing the top. Inside the tube was a small paper scroll. I examined the glass tube closely. I saw something printed on the paper but I could not decipher the words.

"What is that?", Laura asked.

"You got me.", I answered.

The cork was pushed into the tube real tight. I tried wiggling the cork to loosen it from the top of the tube and then it came off with a loud pop noise. I turned the tube upside down and let the scroll fall out into my hand. While I was still holding the tube, I unrolled the scroll and printed on the paper was the following statement:

RETURN

ALL OF THIS IS A DREAM.

"What? I don't understand.", I disclosed. Laura grabbed the scroll from me and she read it.
"All of this is a dream? What does that mean?", Laura echoed. Henry grabbed the scroll from her and read it.
"How is this the key to the universe?", Henry remarked. Henry looked up at us and then he focused his attention on something behind us. Laura and I turned around and we saw a woman with long dark hair and glasses dressed in a gray pantsuit walking towards us.
"Hello there!", the woman said as she kept walking towards us.
"Hello." I cautiously said. She stopped and looked at all three of us.
"I see that you figured out the riddle.", the woman acknowledged.
"Yeah, we all did.", I told the woman.
"Well, let me be the first to say Congratulations! In the 200 years that the town of Return has existed, you three are the first to figure out the riddle! As a reward for solving the riddle, the mayor and his wife would like to see all of you personally.", the woman told us.
I looked at Laura and Henry and they all looked pleased so I decided to go along with it.
"Alright, lead the way.", I agreed.
"Excellent! Follow me.", instructed the woman.
The three of us followed the woman as we walked across the town square and making our way around the

remnants from the festival. I noticed other people in the square staring at us as we were walking by. I wasn't sure why.

All I did was figure out a riddle. It's not like I killed anybody.

We got to the road in the middle of steady traffic and all the cars stopped. The drivers seemed to be staring at us as we crossed. We made it to the other side and then went up the front stairs of the town hall. The woman opened the door for us and then said "Please, come on in. They're waiting for you."

Laura, Henry and I entered the building and the doors closed with a thundering boom.

TWENTY-TWO

Laura and I were holding hands in the lobby of the building with Henry right behind us. The lobby was brightly illuminated with the sunlight. The woman walked up the staircase in front of us and we followed. After we climbed that set, we turned and went up another set of stairs then we reached the next floor. The woman took a left and we followed her down a white hallway with blue carpeting. Oddly, there was no décor of any kind on the walls of the hallway. We rounded another corner on our left and approached a set of white double doors.

We entered through the doors and into a waiting

room with a desk. The woman went over to the desk and sat down. She picked up the phone and pushed a button.

"They're out here and ready for you.", she said into the mouthpiece. She listened to the voice on the other end and then she hung up the phone. "The mayor will see you now. Just go through those double doors to your right.", she advised.

"Thanks.", I said to the secretary. I walked over to one of the doors and reached for the knob. I turned it and opened the door. The three of us entered into the corner of a large office. Henry closed the door behind us.

There was an American flag on a stand. The walls were decorated with various black and white photos. At the opposite corner of the room was a giant mahogany desk accompanied by a brown leather chair. The back of the chair was facing us and the occupant was looking outside through the window, enjoying the view of the town square.

"Hi, Mr. Mayor! I'd like to introduce you to my boyfriend, Charlie!", Laura happily said.

"Good morning, Mr. Mayor.", I politely greeted.

"Hello, my boy.", the Mayor said.

That was the voice I heard over the speakers yesterday at the festival. Why does that voice sound familiar? I know I've heard it before. The mayor stood up from his chair then turned around and faced us.

I saw his face. He was staring right at me.
It can't be.
How is that possible?
I was frozen with a mix of shock and fear but I also

felt a tornado of emotions stirring up inside me.

"Dad?", I said.

"My son.", replied my father. He went around the desk and walked toward me. He looked exactly the same as the last time I saw him. Another door in the office to my left opened. A woman walked through it and I felt more emotions rising up from within me as I instantly recognized who it was. I felt my eyes begin to float in my sockets.

"Mom?", I sniffled. She also looked like that she hadn't aged a day.

I looked over at Laura and saw her eyes wide open with both of her hands covering her mouth as she had a look of disbelief on her face. Henry put his arm around her, also surprised at what was happening. I turned back to my parents, my dead parents, and they walked over to me. They both stood in front of me happily smiling.

I couldn't believe I was seeing them.

"How? How is this possible? Both of you are dead!", I exclaimed.

"Honey, we're here because you want us here.", explained my mom.

I didn't understand.

"Of course, I want both of you around. I miss you both horribly but how can you both be here now?", I asked them.

"It's because of you, son. You want us here.", my father divulged.

I thought about what he said and then the weight of what he said started to have an impact on me. I got a sour feeling that began to churn in my gut. I feared the worse. What was in the box was indeed very heavy.

"Am I... dead?", I asked them.

"It's complicated.", my father stated. He then appended that statement with, "You're not quite dead but you're not quite alive either."

I lost it and I started crying. The tears were free flowing down my face. My mother and father hugged me and I put my face into my mother's shoulder. All the pain, sorrow and sadness over the last 18 years of my life just came out of me like flood waters breaking through a dam. The images of the funeral seemed to be just as fresh in my mind as the day it occurred. Yet, I was somehow in the loving embrace of my parents again. I was loudly sobbing and I became congested.

My mother was comforting me again and I felt protected and secure as if we were a family again. "There, there. It's perfectly alright. Let it all out, Honey.", said my mother.

"You're both here!", I wept.

Henry walked up to us and handed me a tissue.

"Here you go, kid.", he offered. I took the tissue from Henry then blew my nose into it and soaked up my snot. "Gross.", I said. Both of my parents chuckled. "You always were funny.", my mom told me.

I wiped the tears from my eyes with my sleeve. I balled up the tissue and threw it into a nearby trash can.

I looked at my parents then I asked, "What happens now?"

RETURN

My father rested his hand on my shoulder. "Charlie, don't you worry about a thing. You control what goes on here... to a degree.", my father said.

"What do you mean 'I control what goes on here'?", I asked.

"Return is your world. You control everything, like I said, to a degree.", he told me.

"So this whole town is my creation?", I questioned.

"Yes.", my dad confirmed.

"The box? The environments? The books in the library and the history of the town?"

"Yes to all of those things. It's how you make sense of everything."

"The people?"

"Well, as for the people, that's also complicated.", my father admitted.

"So where am I really now?", I asked.

"I'm sorry, Charlie. I don't know that.", disclosed my father.

"Am I still in my car?"

"It's possible but I don't know that.", he repeated.

"Fortunately for you though, you are in a position to go back. We will be a family again some day but it's your decision on if you want to make that happen sooner or later.", my mother addressed.

"I miss you both so much. I want to be with both of you again.", I said and the tears began to pour out of me again.

"We miss you too, my boy.", spoke my father.

Henry handed me another tissue and I cleaned up

more of my bodily fluids that were percolating from the orifices of my face. I balled up that tissue and threw it into the trash can without actually aiming.

"Honey, we want you to be with us but we care more about your life and your happiness over ours. You have so much life left to live.", urged my mother.

"We don't have our lives anymore. There's nothing we can do about that. You on the other hand, you can live that life that we've always wanted for you. Maybe someday even you will become a father and you will know how we felt when you were born.", my father declared.

"We are so proud of the man you've become, Charlie, and we will always love you. We are both so sorry that we couldn't be around to see you grow up and be there for you in the good times and the bad times. I know that we do not live on in your life but we will always live on in your heart.", assured my mother.

"Mr. Mayor", began Henry, "I just want to let you know that your boy is a good kid. He turned out very well considering the situation he was thrown into early in his life."

"Thank you, Henry.", praised my father.

I felt another hand on my shoulder. I turned around and Laura was there. "Charlie, I want you to know that I think you are a great human being. I will be there for you and I also love you.", she confessed.

I smiled at her and said, "I love you, too." I turned towards her then hugged her and kissed her right there in

front of Henry and my parents.
    It felt amazing to hear her say that and it felt right to say that to her at that moment. I did love her.
    Although, I just had a strange feeling like I just had an epiphany.
    Did I love Laura or did I love Heidi?
    Instantly, I felt this uneasiness within me growing in the pit of my stomach.
    I looked outside and noticed that it seemed to be getting dark. The sunlight was slowly vanishing and it was growing dim. I broke from the group hug and looked out of the window. The sky was becoming dark. I looked at the clock on the wall and it was only a little bit before noon.
    What is going on?
    "Is there a storm coming?", I asked. Everyone walked over to me and looked out the window.
    "I don't know, son. Like I said before, you control this world and what happens in it.", my father reminded me.
    I looked down at the ground. I saw that all the cars were gone except for Henry's truck and there was no traffic on the roads. None. The mess from the festival was also gone. I also did not see any people outside. They were gone too.
    "Where did everybody go? A bunch of people watched the three of us walk into this building like we were going to the electric chair and poof! Now no one is around! Just gone without a trace!"
    I walked away from the window and walked towards the double doors that went back towards the waiting room. I

opened the doors and the secretary was also gone. I was getting a little freaked out.

"Where the hell did she go?!", I raised my voice.

My mother walked up to me and lightly grabbed my shoulders.

"Honey, we don't know where she went. You are in control of what is going on.", she said.

"What do you mean, Mom?!", I shouted.

"Honey, calm down. Things could get bad if you do not calm down."

I walked away from her and exited the waiting room. I went back down the white hallway. I saw Laura, Henry and my parents following me out of the office and I went back downstairs. The lobby was no longer brightly illuminated by the sunlight. I walked up to the front door and opened it. I could see that it was getting darker by the minute and I heard a quiet but unusual noise coming from somewhere outside that seemed to be getting louder.

TWENTY-THREE

    I walked outside and down the front steps. I looked toward the left and saw that the sun was still shining in the sky. Then I looked right and I saw that the sky was as black as night and as ominous as death. I walked across the street and into the newly cleared town square.

    I thought I faintly heard some voices. Possibly some indistinct screaming or crying but I looked all around me. I did not see a single person around except for my parents, Laura and Henry. They, however, we're not talking. They were just following where I was going. I had no idea where that sound of distressed voices was coming from or where everyone went. All the citizens in Return just disappeared.

    I heard another strange noise that was occurring behind me. I turned around and noticed that it was coming from the direction of the black sky. Even though I was standing about a mile or so away from the lake, I could see a clear distant view of the horizon from here as I looked down the road that led to the farm. The horizon was an extremely deep black and it looked like the sky was changing shape. Laura walked up to me and she began to look at what I was seeing. Henry and my parents joined us.

    "What is that?", Laura curiously said.

    "What is the sky doing?", Henry asked. I kept staring at it and it seemed like the sky was coming closer but then I realized that something far worse than the sky was coming this way.

    "Oh, shit. That's not the sky.", I asserted and I began to worry.

    "What is it?!", demanded Laura.

    I kept staring at the spectacle that was coming towards us and saw the foaming crest of a moving wall of water.

    "That's the lake. That's a massive tidal wave.", I told her.

    We were all hypnotized at the enormous tidal wave that was growing in height and was moving closer to us.

    I felt someone grab me and I was suddenly looking at my mom as she was holding me.

    "Charlie, you need to get out of here.", she warned.

    "Why? Why do I have to go?", I insisted.

RETURN

"You can't stay.", my father said.

"I want to stay. I don't... I don't want the both of you to leave me again.", I stammered.

"Honey, there's nothing you can do for us. You have to go. You have to leave us.", she spoke.

I felt those tears coming back again.

"I can't. It hurts so much being without both of you.", I sobbed as I began to sniffle again. My father put his hand on my shoulder.

"*Son*, if you don't go, you will die! You need to live, for both of us! Please!", begged my father with urgency.

"You can live on without us. I believe in you. You're so strong and brave. Remember, we live on in your heart and we will always love you.", my mother encouraged.

"This goodbye isn't forever. You will see us again someday." my father assured me.

I wrapped my arms around both of my parents and they held me in their arms one last time.

"I love you both, too.", I cried as the tears began to flow again. I stepped away from my mother and father then wiped my tears away.

I felt the town begin to exhibit a slight tremble. I felt the vibrations beneath my feet. Within a few seconds, the trembling seemed to increase to a small earthquake.

"What is happening?!", I hollered.

"Charlie! We need to go!", Laura yelled and I saw her and Henry running towards the truck. I looked back at my parents.

"Goodbye, my boy.", said my father.

"Goodbye, Honey.", said my mother.

I finally said the words that I never got to say to them before.

"Goodbye, Mom. Goodbye, Dad."

    I turned around and ran back to the truck as fast I could. Henry started up the truck. The ground cracked in front of me and began to separate. I jumped over the small chasm and got my footing over the other side. I ran into the street and I hopped into the back of the truck. I looked back over at my parents who were standing in the town square. My father had his arm around my mother and they both smiled and waved at me.

    The entire town began to violently shake. Buildings began to fall apart. I heard the sound of the tidal wave coming closer. Light posts and fire hydrants were shooting up into the air from the ground and water began spraying. The iron box was actually swaying back and forth. I hammered my fist on the top of the truck a couple times.

    "Go!", I yelled.

    Henry took off like a bat out of hell. He sped down the road. I was clenching on to the side of the truck as tightly as I could. He flew through the intersection and I saw the road behind us begin to split. We passed by the various establishments on the road and all the windows began to break. He sped past Martha's and the diner just imploded. As he rounded the corner on the left, I saw the gigantic rush of water breach the town square. He sped down this last street and I saw more buildings collapsing. I felt hostile tremors beneath the truck.

RETURN

Henry made a sharp right turn onto the road out of town; the very same road I took to get into town and he floored it. I looked back at the town sign and then the entire town just dropped out of view and into the ground. In an instant, the whole town of Return was swallowed by the Earth. The tidal wave flew over the newly created beach front property and aggressively chased us down the road.

The tidal wave was still coming after us and devouring the ground in its wake. Henry threw the truck into another gear and kept racing the tidal wave. We continued down the desolate road and the tidal wave mowed over the trees along our way.

I saw the trees all around us shaking. One tree was losing its stance and it began to fall in front of us. Henry floored it as I heard the engine rev with more power. The tree came down and we barely dodged it as it landed just behind us.

The wave still pursued us and blasted through the downed tree with an immense force, reducing it to kindling. We were still outrunning the wave but it was gaining on us and it was destroying everything in its path.

Henry kept speeding and finally we were out of the woods and we just had a clear open road in front of us. The wave kept chasing us. Then buildings started appearing on the sides of the road and I recognized them.

I saw my former place of employment. I saw my high school. I saw my parents' old house. I saw my Uncle Greg's house. I saw the bar down the street from my apartment. I saw my apartment building. All of these buildings were lining up on the sides of the same road.

This isn't making sense. Why are all these here?

"Charlie!", called Laura. I went to the back window of the truck and she was looking at me concerned for my safety.

"Laura!", I acknowledged.

"Don't you leave me!", she yelled.

"Never!", I answered.

"I love you!", she told me.

"I love you, too!", I told her.

I heard an enormous rumbling close by. I looked forward past Laura and a loud crash of water exploded upwards from the ground a short distance in front of us on the road. There was another tidal wave so large that it appeared to eclipse the sun and it was rushing directly at us. Henry was speeding directly towards it. I looked back at Laura. She put her hand on the glass and I saw a tear roll down her cheek. I put my hand on the glass right where her hand was and I felt such an immense sadness building up within me.

The waves collided with the truck and I was knocked out of the bed of the truck. I was encapsulated in the water. The waves shook me around and pulverized me as if I had become trash in the ocean. I lost my direction and I could not see where I was going. I just saw an endless sea of blue.

I got turned in one direction and I finally saw the truck below me. The waves were pushing me farther away from the truck. I reached out for the truck screaming in an unfathomable agony but the distance between the truck and

RETURN

I was just increasing.
I couldn't save them.
I lost my parents again.
I lost the woman I love again.
I'm submerged in a flood of biblical proportions with very little air.
So, this is it.
This is how I'm going to die.
I've avoided water for so long and I'm going to drown.
What's left that's worth fighting for?
Fuck it.
Kill me quickly. Please...
Another rush of water spun me around again and I lost sight of the truck. I wanted to breathe and I couldn't. My chest was constricted and I was suffocating. I was being pushed away from the ground and towards the top. My vision was losing focus and I had no strength and no will to live left in me. I saw a light above me that was becoming brighter and was reflecting everywhere. Right at the moment where I was just about to give up and just let myself take the liquid death into my lungs, I felt my face break the surface tension of the water.

TWENTY-FOUR

I woke up. I felt a tear roll down my face. I saw a white ceiling above me and florescent lights were beaming down on me. This felt different. I heard electronic machines that were frantically beeping. I was looking around and saw a nurse that became alarmed.

I heard her yell, "I need a doctor!" then she ran away from me. It seemed like I was in a hospital bed but I was panicking. I was breathing fairly rapidly and I had a tube down my throat.

What is going on? Somebody help me!

I tried to look around but I noticed there was a bandage on my head that slightly obscured part of my view.

RETURN

I looked down at myself and saw that my left arm and my left leg were both in a cast. I felt a catheter in my penis and saw a colostomy bag inserted into my abdomen.

A gentleman with short brown hair and glasses rushed over to me. He looked strangely familiar.

Jack?

The nurse followed behind him. He pulled out a small flashlight and was shining it in my eyes.

He must be the doctor.

He turned off the flashlight and I saw him look at something to my left. "It's okay. Just relax. Breathe slowly. You have a tube in your throat. Relax. Don't try to speak.", the doctor advised. I began to breathe more deeply and calmly per the doctor's instructions. The beeping on the machine began to slow down.

"That's good, Charlie. Good. Just relax.", said the doctor.

I continued to slowly breathe and I felt myself gradually relaxing despite all the various devices inserted in me.

"Charlie, I'm Doctor Collins. Blink twice if you can understand me.", the doctor ordered.

I blinked twice.

"Good, Charlie. You are in the Intensive Care Unit of Millard Fillmore Hospital. You were in a car accident and have been here since then recovering from your injuries. Blink twice if you understand what I just told you."

I blinked twice again.

"Good, Charlie. There will be plenty of time later to

talk about your prognosis. Right now, just relax. I'll be right back.", spoke Doctor Collins.

The doctor exited the room and the nurse stayed there with me. I saw her looking at something next to the bed. I assumed she was probably analyzing my vitals displaying on the machine. I saw her lift up the IV drip and insert a syringe into the tube.

"Here, this should relax you and help with any discomfort.", the nurse commented. I saw her press down the plunger. Within a couple minutes, I felt more comfortable. I started to feel a little drowsy but it took the edge off of some of the pain. I heard the steps of a group of people nearing the door and then enter the room. Doctor Collins came into view.

"Charlie, you have some visitors.", Doctor Collins announced. The doctor stepped aside and my Uncle Greg walked by him.

"Oh my God, Charlie! You're awake!", cried my uncle. I saw him cover his mouth and I saw him begin to cry. I've never seen him cry before. He walked over to the right side of the bed and held my right hand.

"It's okay, pal. You're going to be okay.", he assured me. I heard slow steps approaching my bed. I looked over in the direction of where they were coming from and I couldn't believe my eyes.

It was Heidi.

"Charlie!", she wept. She started to cry so hard. She came over to me and kissed me on the cheek.

"I didn't think you were going to wake up! I've been

here all along and I was freaking out over what the machines were doing just now and the nurse pulled me away! I just... I love you so much!", she told me with sniffles.

I love you, too. I wish I could say that to her right now.

She reached for my left hand and held it.

"We're here for you now. Don't worry about anything. Just rest.", she reassured.

I saw tears run down her face and I've never seen her smile so big. She looked so happy to see me.

"What about the tube in his throat?", my uncle asked Doctor Collins.

"We're going to monitor him for a little bit and make sure he's stable before we take it out. Right now, Charlie, just rest. The fact that you woke up is simply a miracle but you're not out of the woods yet.", Doctor Collins informed us.

I looked at him and blinked at him twice. He smiled.

"Very good.", he smirked. He looked at my Uncle and said, "Just notify the nurse if you need anything. I'll come back in a little bit to check on him." I saw the doctor exit the room.

I looked up at the ceiling and shut my eyes. I still felt the touch of my Uncle Greg and Heidi on my hands. I laid there as relaxed as I could be without disturbing any of the equipment attached to me.

My eyes felt sensitive to the light in the room so I shut them for a bit.

I began to think of the farm again. I was standing in the field near the edge of the cliff just looking at the lake and that endless horizon.

"Charlie."

I turned around and I saw Laura one last time dressed up in her cowgirl attire and wearing her white Stetson. She walked up to me and said, "I miss you." I hugged her and she hugged me back.

I missed her touch. This experience felt different than before. It now felt like a dream.

"I miss you, too... but... you're someone I made up. You are a part of me but you're not real and I have to move on.", I told her.

"I know. I will always live on in your heart as Laura just like Heidi lives on in your life now. Heidi was with you the whole time while you were here and you saw her as me.", she admitted.

"I realize that now but I want you to know that you will always have a place in my heart. I won't forget you. I am grateful for you and her for getting me through this ordeal.", I praised.

She put her hand on my face and looked into my eyes.

"Please, just kiss me one last time.", she said.

I leaned in to kiss her and our lips touched one last time.

I opened my eyes.

I was looking up at the ceiling in my room. I heard the television and looked over at the screen. I saw my Uncle watching some action movie. The hero was shooting a machine gun and he looked familiar.

Henry?

I moved my arm and tapped the side of the bed. My uncle looked over at me and said, "Hey pal, I see you're up. Let me go get the doctor." My uncle exited the room and left the television on. I watched a little more of the action movie as explosions were happening on screen then my uncle, Heidi, and the doctor walked into the room.

Heidi grabbed the remote for the television and then turned it off.

"I'm so sick of that movie. It's been on so much recently.", she revealed then set the remote on the bed.

I saw Doctor Collins look at the monitor. He looked at me and declared, "Your vitals are looking good. I'm going to remove this tube. This will be a little uncomfortable but it'll be out before you know it."

I felt him remove the strap from around my head and the tube became loose. He slowly pulled out the tube. I felt it slide out with all my saliva and started to gag on the tube. It was finally out of my throat and I coughed up some phlegm.

"Just breathe.", instructed Doctor Collins.

I was breathing on my own. It felt great to have that tube finally out.

"How are you feeling?", asked Doctor Collins.

"I'm starving.", I quietly answered.

The doctor smiled.

"That's a good sign. I'll have the nurse bring you some food shortly.", Doctor Collins approved.

"Charlie, the doctor is going to explain your situation to you and we're right here for you.", Heidi chimed in. She grabbed my hand.

"Charlie", Doctor Collins started, "you sustained quite a head injury. You had some trauma to your skull and needed staples, four specifically. You were in a coma for twenty-three days."

"Holy shit. Oh. Sorry for the language.", I mumbled.

"Don't worry. That's an appropriate response.", quipped Doctor Collins.

"Your left arm and your left leg are both broken in two different places. Due to the nature of your injuries, including your head, physical therapy will be necessary for your body in order for it to get back to functioning normally. We'll eventually go over a plan for rehabilitation but for now the plan is to just rest. Doctor's orders.", Doctor Collins clarified.

"Okay, Doc. Sounds like a plan.", I complied.

"Very good. If you need anything else, the call button is on the railing of the bed next to your right hand. The nurse will be able to help you with what you need. I'll come by again tomorrow and check up on you. Okay?"

I nodded in approval. "Good. I'll get the nurse to bring you some food.", Doctor Collins told me.

"Thanks, Doc.", said my uncle. The doctor nodded and exited the room. Heidi pulled up a chair and sat down next to me. She gently placed her hand on my left hand sticking out of the cast and looked at me.

"It was scary before you woke up out of the coma. Your vitals were going a little crazy. I wasn't sure what was happening. I was panicking like mad. It really is a miracle that now you're back and you're talking.", she confessed.

"The doctor said that most comatose patients generally don't wake up after about a month. It truly is amazing that you woke up.", added Uncle Greg.

"I missed you both so much I had to return.", I told her. She smiled wide and a tear rolled down her cheek. "I missed you, too. We both did.", she said. She pulled a tissue out of her purse and wiped the tear away. She clenched on to the tissue, seeming to be ready for more that may come.

"Don't fill up too much on hospital food. Thanksgiving is in a couple days. I'll bring you some great food and I'll be spending it here with you.", Heidi mentioned.

"Me too, pal. It really takes on a whole new meaning this year. Both of us were here a lot watching over you while you were sleeping. I'll be sticking around to help you out with what you need now that you're up. Work can wait.", my uncle stated.

I felt grateful for that. It warmed my heart.

"Thank you for watching over me. Both of you. I love you both.", I said with overwhelming gratitude.

Uncle Greg reached for my hand and Heidi kissed me on the lips. "We love you, too.", she told me.

I am here for another day on Earth.
I knew what I was thankful for this year.

TWENTY-FIVE

    I was finally moved out of the Intensive Care Unit and into a normal room. I sat up in the hospital bed and was finally able to wear a sweatshirt that Heidi brought me from home. My arm and leg were newly out of their casts for the past couple days and the afflicted areas of my limbs were securely wrapped with bandages. It felt nice to finally get that hospital gown off of me. Thanksgiving had come and gone. Eating the meal here was a bit awkward but it was delicious as I quickly got pretty sick of the hospital food. Dean fired me from Red Wheel Products but I didn't care. I knew I could eventually find a new job.

RETURN

I love food so much maybe I should get into the restaurant business.

Anyway, it was the middle of the week before Christmas and I was going to be discharged in a day or two. I had been looking forward to having a nice holiday at home with loved ones.

Heidi was sitting next to me and we were watching *Wheel of Fortune*. The current turn belonged to some jackass who kept buying vowels for the puzzle and was not guessing the most frequently used consonants. We both had the impression that he didn't realize that buying vowels costs money.

The jackass on the TV reminded me of Tyler, and not the one from Return. Now I had a certain thought on my mind and I needed closure.

"Heidi?", I asked her.

"Yeah?", she responded.

"Why are you back with me?", I asked her. She picked the remote up off the bed and muted the television. She hung her head and seemed reluctant to look at me.

"I'm sorry to bring up old wounds but it's really bothering me. You did tell me during that fight that you did not want to have a life together if I was going to act like the way I did towards your old friends. You told me that you didn't want to see me again. I'm not trying to start another fight but I need to know.", I explained. She hesitantly looked at me.

"I didn't want to bring up the fight because you were recovering from the accident and it was such a horrible incident. Charlie, you were completely right and I'm very, very sorry. I'm so sorry I did not believe you before when you told me that it was not you in that photo. I felt so guilty while you were laying in the hospital bed. After I said all that to you, I was so afraid that I was never going to speak to you again so I could rectify what happened. I was crying so hard when the machines were going crazy right before you woke up because I thought you were going to die right there in front of me." She lowered her head again and began to cry. I reached for her hand.

"Don't be upset, Honey. I'm sorry too. I should've never stormed out of the apartment like that. I wouldn't have gotten into the accident if I never left. I'm sorry for putting you through all that emotional turmoil." Heidi looked back at me and smiled as she wiped her away her tears. She sniffled.

"Well, don't you worry about Tyler. We are not friends anymore. He is a sociopathic asshole and I'm never going to speak to him again.", she adamantly said.

"Really? What happened?", I asked as I was very intrigued by what I missed.

"He was trying to break us up to get back with me. I knew he was lying when he sent me a photo of you and another girl at some club being very intimate together.", she explained. She reached into her purse and pulled out her phone. She was searching through it and showed me the photograph. It was obviously an altered photograph. It showed a woman kissing a man on the cheek with my pasted on face and she was grabbing his crotch.

"That is definitely not me! That has to be photoshopped!", I protested.

"I know it's not you. I'll get to that. When I got this, you had already been in the hospital for a couple days. The night he sent this to me, I was here at the hospital with you. He told me that he just took this picture at a club downtown. Right there, I knew he was lying because I didn't tell him that you were in the hospital. Also, I looked at the photograph again. Look at his right hand.", she instructed then pointed at it.

I looked at the photograph. There was a dark birthmark on the side of his hand right near the knuckle on his pinky.

I don't have a birthmark there. That's not me.

"I looked at your right hand when you were in the coma. That's not your hand.", she finished.

"You clever little minx. Well, what happened after that?"

"I called him out on his lies and told him to go fuck himself. I also told him if he contacts me again, that I will ruin his social life. I thought being a little vague about it was the best thing to do."

"You have something embarrassing on him, don't you?"

"I don't know what you're talking about.", she said then winked at me. She picked the remote up and turned the sound of the television back on. I decided to let her have her fun and keep her secret.

Uncle Greg walked in the room with a manilla folder in one hand and a plastic bag in the other. "Hey, you two.", as he greeted us.

"Hey.", I answered.

"Hi, how are you?", acknowledged Heidi.

"Here you go, pal.", said Uncle Greg. He handed me the bag. I opened it up and he brought me a couple burritos from this popular fast food chain around the area called Mighty Taco. Don't knock it until you've tried it. It's awesome.

"You brought me Mighty Taco?! Oh, I love you.", I happily said.

Uncle Greg laughed. He took his coat off and set it on a chair on the side of the bed opposite of Heidi. He sat down in that same chair and looked up at Wheel of Fortune.

"Captain Morgan Freeman.", Uncle Greg said as he figured out the puzzle and the jackass on the television kept buying vowels for the puzzle.

I looked at the puzzle and Uncle Greg was right.

"Oh, yeah. Nice.", I affirmed.

"So, I thought you might want to take a look at this.", asserted Uncle Greg. He handed me the folder and I took it from him.

"What's this?", I asked.

"It's the police report from the accident.", he claimed.

I was surprised by that. I opened it up and I saw the report in front of me. I began to read it.

The subject's vehicle swerved off the road at high speed and hit a tree. The vehicle then appeared to continue to roll downhill after

RETURN

sustaining the initial impact. The vehicle hit another tree on the way down and eventually slid into a boulder at the bottom of the hill causing the vehicle to stop in an upside down position. The tracks on the ground and the damage to the car and environment are consistent with these events.

I stopped reading the report then lifted it to find photographs of my destroyed car. The front of the car was smashed in like it was a tin can. The driver side door and the roof were also smashed in. The driver side window was broken and the windshield was cracked. The front axle was broken. I saw another angle of the accident and it looked like the body of the car was slightly curved in the shape of a crescent moon.

"Wow. I survived that?"

"Yeah, pal. Quite unbelievable, isn't it?", admitted Uncle Greg.

"Well, I won't be driving again for a while anyway. Plenty of time to decide what type of car I should get.", I reckoned.

I put the report and the photos back in the folder and closed it. I set the folder on the bed. I laid back in my bed and exhaled with a large breath. Seeing those pictures just put me in a state of disbelief.

They were right. I was lucky to be here.

I sat back up then reached into the bag and opened the wrapper on one of the burritos. I bit into that meaty goodness and it was such a welcome break from the hospital food. I took a few more large bites out of it as if it was contraband. In a hospital, it probably was but I didn't care what they thought. I survived a brutal car accident and I just wanted to enjoy my burrito. I swallowed that last bite and tossed the wrapper in the bag.

"Hello?", a voice called into my room.

I put the bag of food under my blanket. It was my nurse, Kim, and she had a wheelchair for me. I waved at her and she waved back. Heidi moved out of the way to make room for the wheelchair. She wheeled it next to the bed and locked the brakes on the chair.

"Hi, Charlie.", Kim announced.

"Hi, Kim.", I greeted her.

"It's time for your physical therapy session.", Kim reported.

"Alrighty.", I complied.

Uncle Greg walked over to the other side of the bed and helped the nurse and I with me moving my legs over the side of the bed. Uncle Greg took my good arm and put it around him. He also held me by my other armpit. Kim and Heidi grabbed my legs and helped me into the chair. I got my butt into the chair and rested my feet on the foot plates. Kim unlocked the breaks and grabbed a hold of the chair. I looked back at Heidi and Uncle Greg.

"I'll be back in a while.", I told them.

"We'll be here, pal.", promised Uncle Greg.

Kim wheeled me out of the room and we turned right down the hallway. She wheeled me down the hallway and we turned a corner. We headed towards the elevators.

"How are you, today?", asked Kim.

RETURN

"I'm good. Not much discomfort at all.", I replied.

"Good to hear.", she said.

She pushed a button and the door opened. Kim wheeled me into the elevator and she stepped in then turned me around to face the doors. She pushed a button for the first floor. The doors closed and I felt the elevator go down.

"Do I smell Mighty Taco?", Kim mused.

Oh boy.

"I don't think so.", I responded as calmly as I could.

The lift stopped and the doors opened. Kim wheeled me out of the elevator and we turned left.

"You should be getting out of here real soon. Excited?", asked Kim.

"Absolutely. I'm looking forward to Christmas dinner.", I told her.

"I bet you are. One can only take so much hospital food.", she added.

I chuckled at her remark. We continued down the hall and then Kim wheeled me into a room on my left.

There was a woman in the room wearing a yellow polo shirt and khakis with dark long hair tied up in a pony tail looking at a patient chart. I assumed she was looking at mine. She didn't look like the usual physical therapist that I started working with in these sessions.

"I got your two o'clock here.", Kim said.

The woman turned around. She was older but she also looked familiar.

Martha?

"Thanks.", the woman said. Kim stopped the chair and locked the brakes on the chair. Kim left the room.

"Hi, Charlie. My name is Anna. How are you?", she inquired.

"I'm alright. How are you?", I asked her.

"I'm well. Listen before we start, I want to ask you something. Is your mother Cynthia Denton?" I was surprised by the question.

"Yes. How do you know that?", I politely questioned her.

"We were great friends. I've actually met you before but I haven't seen you since, well, your parents' funeral. It's been so long. You're all grown up."

I remembered her now. The woman in the black dress and the black veil holding my hand in front of my mother's casket.

"Oh my God. I thought you looked familiar.", I told her.

"Your name rang a bell so I had to ask. It is so good to see you."

"Likewise. I did wonder what happened with you since then.", I said.

"Well, as you can see, I'm a physical therapist and I work a lot. How about you? Despite the circumstances, it looks like you turned out just fine."

"I think so. I have my girlfriend and she's wonderful. I love her to death. I am unemployed at the moment but that's fine because I'm more concerned with getting better. My uncle and I are pretty close, too."

"Gregory? How is he? I haven't seen him in so long. I've always liked him.", she confided.

RETURN

"He's good. He's upstairs visiting in my room.", I mentioned.

"Yeah?", she beamed.

"Yeah, he's been keeping me company and helping me out during my stay. You should go say hi. I bet he would like that.", I told her.

"I tell you what. After we are done with the session, I will personally take you upstairs and we'll all do some catching up.", Anna said.

"I like that idea.", I responded.

"Good. Let's get started with some stretching. I want you to start with your left foot and rotate it twenty times."

Anna picked up my leg and held it. I began to rotate my left foot and fortunately for me, there was no discomfort in performing that action.

"Thank you.", I said.

"Anytime, Darlin'."

Now I want some chicken noodle soup.

TWENTY-SIX

    Five months of gut-wrenching physical therapy later and I was finally walking on my own. It was Memorial Day weekend and Heidi and I rented a cabin out in the woods for the long weekend plus a few extra days for a nice vacation. The plan was to do as little work as possible. Going through that physical therapy was the toughest thing I've endured.

    I also invited my Uncle Greg and Anna to join us. I'm glad I got those two together. When they saw each other for the first time in a long time, they seemed to pick up right where they left off. It was undeniable that they were good together and it's been a long time since I've seen my uncle that happy. I could tell he was infatuated with Anna.

We just finished breakfast. Anna made all of us pancakes and they were damn good. She put blueberries in them. Just delicious. I walked into the bedroom and decided to get dressed and go just check out the wilderness. Heidi hopped in the shower. I threw on a pair of jeans, a T-shirt and my sneakers.

I looked in my bag and found my compass along with a little special something.

Take them.

I put both objects in my front pockets. I double checked what I had on my person and made sure I had everything I needed.

I walked out of the bedroom then opened the bathroom door and stuck my head inside. "Hey, I'm going to do some exploring around outside.", I spoke.

"I'll be out there shortly.", Heidi responded from the shower.

I closed the bathroom door and walked through the kitchen. I saw Uncle Greg sitting at the table finishing his morning coffee and reading some news article on his laptop.

Having wi-fi out in the wilderness is a funny concept.

Anna was finishing with the dishes. Uncle Greg saw me passing through as I was heading out the back door.

"Hey, pal. What are you up to?", he asked.

"I'm thinking of just going for a little walk around the area. I'll probably do a little exploring and get familiar with our surroundings. I'll be back in a little while.", I told him.

"Sounds good, pal. Give me the scoop when you get

back.", he stated.

"Will do. See you guys later.", I said.

"Have fun.", spoke Anna.

I exited out the back door and onto the back deck.

It is perfect weather out here.

There were sunny skies and the temperature was just right, between warm and cool. I walked down the steps and turned right. The property slightly sloped downward as I walked away from the deck and I headed towards the woods that were behind the cabin. Right when I was about to reach those woods, I noticed to my left and not that far away there was a very large pond, or a lake, depending on your perspective of things.

I don't know why but I felt drawn to it so I headed towards the pond. As I approached the pond, I noticed an empty dock. I went over towards the dock and walked onto it. I made my way towards the edge and stopped. I took in the whole view of this raw scene of nature. Calling it beautiful was selling it short. I also had the realization that I was actually comfortable where I was standing. I wasn't freaking out. There was no uneasiness in my stomach. There was just serenity and calm. I couldn't remember the last time where I felt like this around grandiose bodies of water.

Henry was right. I couldn't live in fear of the unknown. That's no way to live.

I stood at the edge of the dock. I took off my sneakers and socks then put them to the side. I sat down on the edge and dipped my feet in the water. The water was a little cold but I got acclimated to the temperature within a minute.

RETURN

I still felt okay and relaxed. I just looked up and it was so clear out. I heard birds chirping.

Did I finally get over this, which I now declared, ridiculous fear?

No. Not yet.

I stood up and took off my jeans and my T-shirt. I set them next to my sneakers. I stood there in my boxers just staring at the water. There was a gentle breeze against my bare back. I took a couple steps backwards. I dashed towards the edge and leaped into the water with a cannonball. I crashed through the liquid fear and let it embrace me.

Fuck that fear.

I remained motionless under the water. I opened my eyes and looked around. I wanted to keep this moment in my mind. After a few seconds, I swam back up and took in oxygen again. I kept kicking and moving my arms, keeping myself afloat with control of my emotions. I felt an enormous smile form on my face and I crowed with triumph.

Now I was over this ridiculous fear.

I heard a quick loud movement of footsteps on the dock behind me. I turned around and saw Heidi rushing to me.

"Charlie! You're in the water!", she said with a tone of concern in her voice.

"I'm fine! Don't worry!", I jovially told her. She seemed surprised by the answer but when she saw how happy I was then she let out a smile. I could tell that she knew what I was doing. I swam towards the dock and climbed up a ladder that was attached to the dock.

    I finished my ascension, happy with what I just did and happy to see Heidi. I looked at her then did a double take for a moment. I almost mistook her for Laura. I noticed that she was sporting the Western boots that she wore at the Halloween party along with her jeans and a Buffalo Sabres T-shirt. She was indulging in her inner country girl mood.

    "So why did you go in the water?"

    "I felt I had to. It was time to deal with it."

    "That's great. I'm happy for you.", she said then she kissed me. I reached for my jeans and began to put them on as I was still soaking wet.

    Had I known I would've done this, I would've brought a towel. Whatever. I'm on vacation.

    "I see you're rocking the shit kickers today.", I told her.

    "Of course. I love these boots. They make me look taller and they're a hell of a lot more comfortable than heels.", she replied.

    I'm glad I brought what I needed. I feel now is a perfect time.

    "Well, I love how they look on you. I figure you may want to wear this with them as well."

    I got down on my left knee and pulled the ring out of my pocket as I was still shirtless and soaking wet. She put her hands over her mouth in complete shock and I could tell she was not expecting this.

    "Oh my God. Oh my God. Charlie, are you asking me what I think you are asking me?", she shrieked as tears began to roll down her face.

"Heidi, I'm here at your mercy. Partially naked and wet as I'm having my own revelation. You were there for me when I needed you and when I wanted you and I intend to do the same for you. We savored our great times and fought through our bad times. So what I am saying is, will you be my wife?", I asked her. I also felt tears well up in me then they began to stream from my sockets but they probably blended in with the water that saturated my body.

She uncovered her mouth and smiled wide at me. More tears streamed down her face and she nodded her head.

"Yes. I would love to be your wife!", she bubbled.

She stuck her hand out and I put the ring on her finger.

I got up off my knee and kissed her. I hugged her then picked her up and spun her around. I screamed at the top of my lungs in complete joy in the middle of the wilderness. I didn't care who heard.

"YES!!!"

I set her back down on the dock and I kissed her again while still holding on to her.

"I love you.", I told her.

"I love you, too.", she said back.

I let her go and I reached down for my shirt. I put that back on and just picked up my sneakers and socks. She grabbed my free hand and we walked off the dock and back on to land.

"We should probably break the news to Greg and

Anna.", suggested Heidi.

"Eh, not yet. Let's take the scenic route and we'll tell them when we return.", I convinced her.

She smiled at me and we went for a stroll around the pond. It was at that moment I felt everything between me and her was setting perfectly into place. Healthy or sick, wealthy or poor, she was who I wanted to be with for the rest of my life. I loved her more than life itself.

I wasn't afraid of what could happen and I did not want to dwell on it. I had to take each minute, each hour and each day for what it was as I found a new philosophy and prerogative on life. I had to savor every moment that passed, good and bad. I needed to cherish those moments to feel that I was alive. In an instant or in a gradual process, I know that this life will eventually end and I do not want to waste it. I was enlightened. I was grateful. I was awake.

EPILOGUE

I burst through the thick double doors and rushed through the Labor and Delivery wing of the hospital. A few yards ahead of me was a kiosk occupied by a couple attendants. I ran up to it and approached the attendants.

"Hi, my wife was just brought in a little bit ago. The name is Heidi Denton.", I told them. One of the nurses behind the kiosk looked at the ledger then turned a page and pointed to an entry.

"Yes, she's in room 320. Keep going straight and it's on the right near the turn.", she declared.

"Thank you.", I acknowledged her. I rushed away from the kiosk and continued down the hall.

"Hey, you have to sign in!", she shouted.

"Sorry, I'm about to be a father!", I yelled back. I ran towards the room and I saw her in bed being wheeled out of the room. Anna came out of the room behind Heidi and was following the gurney.

"Heidi! Anna!"

"Charlie!", Heidi shouted.

Heidi was being wheeled by the nurses around the corner I was approaching. She had to have been going to the delivery room.

"I'm coming!", I yelled down the hall.

I dodged a patient in a wheelchair and maneuvered around a doctor walking towards me. It reminded me of my football days. I rounded the corner and ran into Anna. The doors to the operating room opened as Heidi passed through then they freely swung back and forth after she entered.

"Go. I'll be in her room.", Anna said.

"Thank you." I hugged Anna.

I turned towards the entrance to the delivery room then pushed away one of the doors and entered the room.

"Hey!", one of the nurses objected.

"I'm the father!", I explained to her.

"Okay, but you need to put on scrubs.", she said. She escorted me out of the room. The nurse went over to a drawer and pulled out some for me. I put them on over my clothes. The nurse set a box of latex gloves next to a sink near the door.

"Wash your hands then put these on.", she commanded.

I did as she said then reached into the box and put

them on. I rushed back into the room and reached for Heidi's hand.

"It's okay, baby. I'm here. Just breathe.", I assured her. I tried to comfort her as much as I could.

"I'm breathing. I'm breathing.", she said.

I saw the doctor examining down below.

"What's the status, Doc?", I asked.

"She's starting to crown. Heidi, I need you take a couple deep breaths and then I need you to push, okay?"

Heidi took a couple breaths and then her breathing sped up.

"Okay, push!", the doctor instructed. She strained her face then she tensed up and pushed with a laborious grunt.

"That's good, Heidi. We're not quite there yet.", the doctor stated.

"You're doing great, hun.", I encouraged her as best as I could.

"I need you to push again. Okay?", the doctor ordered. Heidi nodded her head as beads of sweat were flowing down her face.

"You got this, babe.", I told her. I gave her my hand and she clutched it in her surprisingly strong grasp.

"You ready? Push!", commanded the doctor. Heidi tensed up again and pushed. She grabbed my hand much tighter then let out a scream that would put a banshee to shame.

Damn, she is squeezing the shit out of my hand!

She fell back onto the table as she was profusely sweating and breathing heavy.

"You're doing great.", I reassured her. She kept holding my hand with a vice-like grip and I was breathing with her in unison.

"Heidi, the head is out. You're almost done. I need you to push one more time.", directed the doctor.

"Ahh!! This kid is tearing the shit out of my fucking pussy!!", Heidi yelled.

Wow.

"It's okay. It's okay.", I advised her.

"Fuck you, Charlie!", she yelled back.

Hormones and vaginal pain are quite the combination.

"Alright, Heidi. One last push!", instructed the doctor. Heidi tensed up again and gave one more push with an intensity so fierce that I thought I saw a vein bulge from her forehead.

She screamed and then she went limp. I looked at her face and I saw she was exhausted and trying to catch her breath.

I heard a small cry.

Oh my God.

Our child.

"Great, Heidi! The baby is out.", the doctor confirmed. I saw a nurse snip the umbilical cord. Another nurse came over and took the baby from the doctor's arms. I saw her cleaning our baby off.

I looked at Heidi as I felt the biggest smile forming on my face. It looked like she just got kicked by a horse but I sure as shit wasn't going to tell her that. She was still beautiful.

She gave birth to our child. She will always be beautiful.

The nurse came back over to us with our child covered in less of a mess and wrapped in a blanket.

RETURN

"You did it, babe!", I congratulated Heidi.

I saw her just smile. She definitely looked too worn out to respond.

"Congratulations, Mom and Dad. It's a boy!", said the nurse. The nurse handed him to Heidi and she took a hold of our newborn son.

I couldn't believe the moment I was living.

I am a father.
I have a son.
We are a family.
He's been inside of Heidi for nine months and I loved him then but now he has been in the world for two minutes and I already love him beyond comprehension.

I would give my life for him.
I would take life for him.
I would fight to survive for him. In a way, I have already done that but I would do it again in a heartbeat. I don't want him growing up without me or his mother in his life.

Heidi was looking at him with tears coming down her face and she kissed him on the forehead. My tears began to follow suit and I wept with joy.

I wanted to say something to him but an event of this magnitude put me at a loss of words. There was so much of this situation to absorb and so many life-changing prospects to process that it was interfering with my speech.

I collected myself and remembered what my father said. In that moment, I found the words and I let them flow out of me.

"Hello, my boy."

Those words were perfect enough. I finally

understood in that fraction of time the feeling that my father mentioned to me when he became a parent and it was unlike anything I had ever felt before. I wanted more of that feeling then and I still want more of it now.

Thank you, Dad. Thank you, Mom. I know the both of you would be proud grandparents.

It hit me right then and there that my son is now my life. My family is now my life. I encountered the realization that if we happened to be separated in our lifetimes, no matter how far away, that I would do anything to return to them.

RETURN

ABOUT THE AUTHOR

Richie Leyland currently lives in Buffalo, NY. Return is his first novel.

www.richieleyland.com

Thank you for reading my book.

Made in the USA
Columbia, SC
07 January 2018